Hornstone

Major Tim Dillon resigns his army commission in order to run a saloon with his brother, and thinks his fighting days are over. However, after arriving into town just in time to bury his brother, it seems that fate has other plans.

To bring his brother's murderer to justice, and free a town from the grip of evil cattle baron, Stirling Hornstone, he must fight again. Only this time it will be a battle to the death.

This book is to be returned on or before
the last date stamped below.

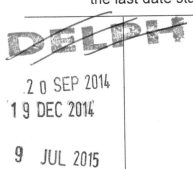

Hornstone

P. McCormac

A Black Horse Western

ROBERT HALE · LONDON

© P. McCormac 2014
First published in Great Britain 2014

ISBN 978-0-7198-1295-8

Robert Hale Limited
Clerkenwell House
Clerkenwell Green
London EC1R 0HT

www.halebooks.com

Typeset by
Derek Doyle & Associates, Shaw Heath
Printed and bound in Great Britain by
CPI Antony Rowe, Chippenham and Eastbourne

1

'Good luck, Captain.' Major Kelly smiled warmly at the tall man clad in buckskins.

The ex-captain stretched his big rangy frame and returned the smile of his onetime senior officer.

'Thanks, Major, but I ain't a captain no more. As of today I'm a civilian.'

The major stuck out his hand and the two men shook.

'I'll miss you, Tim. When trouble brewed and you were there to back me I knew we would come through whatever mess we encountered.'

'Hell, you were the best damn major a man could wish to serve under.'

'We were a good team, Captain Timothy Dillon and Major Thomas Kelly. We sure kept the country safe between us.'

Dillon nodded – a rueful smile on his face. 'Maybe, but we sure did a lot of killing between us also. You think the good Lord will forgive us for all that slaughter?'

'It was for the common good, Tim. The fellas we killed were trying to kill us and hurt a lot of other innocents besides. We executed the ungodly to save ordinary men and women trying to make a decent life for themselves. They wanted to build homes and raise families without having to fight off hostiles while they did so. We did a lot of good for this country. Because of us this is a more civilized place where folk can live in peace and safety.'

'I sure hope when I get to the pearly gates the fellas in charge up there will see it that way. Anyway I'm done with killing now. I done my share and I can hang up my gun and live peaceable.'

'You still set on running a saloon with that brother of yours?'

'Sure am. Dexter is a bit of a wild card. He needs a steady fella like me to make him settle down. I got some savings and he reckons he's building a nest egg, so between us we should be able to buy a darn good outfit. He'll run the gambling side and I'll handle the liquor. Sure make a change for me to give fellas a shot of bourbon instead of a shot of lead.'

The major laughed. 'Mind you send word when you're established. I'll come over there and try out your hospitality. Make sure when you're hiring girls you get some pretty ones. I like them plump.'

They both laughed as old comrades who had been through many skirmishes together and survived. Major Kelly surprised them both when he stepped forward and hugged his former captain. Separating, he saluted smartly.

'You take care, Tim.'

Dillon touched his forehead much more casually than he would have done as a serving soldier, turned to the big gelding tethered to the hitching rail and, putting his foot in the stirrup, smoothly mounted.

'Come on, Monday. We got a mite of travelling to do.'

The horse turned obediently and as it did so a bugle sounded. Dillon looked up in surprise. The courtyard was a hive of activity as uniformed men appeared from all over the fort.

'Form up,' Sergeant O'Grady roared in the voice that vibrated inside soldiers' skulls. 'Two single files.'

Within a short time two lines had formed stretching all the way to the gate. Dillon blinked uncertainly.

'What the hell is going on?' He leaned forward and patted the gelding's neck. 'Nothing for us to worry about, old fella. We're civilians now.' There might have been a discernible note of regret in his voice. 'We better be on our way afore we get caught up in this business.'

He jigged his horse forward, aiming for a course that would avoid interfering in the parade taking place in the courtyard. But he had not gone far before he saw the burly sergeant approaching. Sergeant O'Grady saluted smartly and Dillon had to restrain himself from returning the salute.

'I'm just leaving, Sergeant. I'll not interfere with your parade.'

Sergeant O'Grady's smile exposed tobacco-stained teeth.

'It's not my parade, sir. It's your leaving parade. The men didn't want you to go without the chance to say goodbye.'

Dillon gaped, staring at the two lines of soldiers standing stiffly to attention.

'So if you just ride down the middle of those there lines so the men can see you off in good style, Captain Dillon.'

'Damnit, Sergeant, I ain't a captain no more. And there's no need for all this damn fuss.'

'Just do it for the men, sir.' The sergeant's voice was soft as he spoke. 'They wanted to say goodbye to the best goddamn captain they ever served under.'

The man on the horse couldn't speak. He nodded wordlessly and nudged the horse into a walk. As he rode forward the soldiers, without being ordered, stood stiffly

7

to attention and saluted. The only noise in the fort was the soft plop of hoofs as Monday plodded along the avenue of soldiers. There was a lump in Tim Dillon's throat and he tried to stare straight ahead. Before he reached the gates there was a sudden stirring amongst the troops.

'Three cheers for Captain Dillon.'

With the cheers resounding around the courtyard Dillon urged his mount to a trot as he passed out through the gates of the fort. The ex-soldier was well down the road before he was able to wipe furiously at his eyes.

'Goddamn fool soldiers! Makes a fella wonder what he's leaving.' He drove his heels in to the flanks of his horse and it took off. 'A good hard ride will blow away that army dust. I'm a civilian now. A goddamn saloon owner. I'll stock the best bourbon in Oregon and get the prettiest gals to serve it and I've just thought of a good name for the place. I'll call it Fort Petticoat: Proprietors – Dexter and Timothy Dillon. Yippee! Come on, you mangy old piece of horseflesh. Give a fella a bit of speed. I can't wait to get to meet up with Dexter. The first thing I'm going to do is get as drunk as a skunk and then some.'

The horse stretched itself, glad to be out and running; its long legs easily eating up the miles that were taking the ex-cavalry officer towards a meeting with his brother Dexter and a new life as a civilian.

2

'Dillon, you coming out here or do I have to come in there and drag you out myself?'

The voice was calling from the street outside the Bottom Dollar saloon. The patrons inside looked in the direction of the card school, where four men were sitting.

'That's Grant Hornstone calling you out, Dexter,' Percy Travers said. 'What you going to do?'

Dexter Dillon stared at the pile of dollar bills on the table. In his mid-twenties he was easily the youngest of the card players. All four were dressed in business suits with Dillon's the most elegant. His broadcloth was of the best quality and the stylish cut fitted his broad shoulders and trim figure.

'Somebody go out there and tell him it doesn't have to be like this. I ain't got no quarrel with him.'

'You know that ain't gonna happen. Hornstone is all riled up because you fleeced him of his grubstake.'

'Hell, I'll give him a chance to win it back.'

The other players at the table were shaking their heads.

'He ain't got nothing to bet with. You cleared him out. The son of a bitch reckons you cheated when you won that money. He wants to settle up with you in lead.'

Dexter swore long and luridly. 'How many times during that game did I tell him to ease up and get out while he still had something left? The damn fool wouldn't listen to reason. I offered to finish the game myself and walk away so he could still have money left. He accused me of trying

9

to prevent him winning back his losses. Hell, you can't talk to a headstrong jackass like that. He insisted in staying till his last cent was gone. What sort of a damn fool is that? What the hell was I supposed to do? I ain't his nursemaid. He wouldn't listen to reason, the damn fool. He ain't got the sense of a newborn buffalo calf.'

'Hell, a calf has more sense. It sure knows enough to suckle on its ma.'

The men at the table chuckled.

'Grant sure suckles on his pa's wealth. You can bet your bottom dollar that money came from his pa. Stirling Hornstone is the richest and most powerful man in these parts and maybe the meanest. He sure passed the mean bit on to his son. No one ever got the better of the Hornstones. Or if they did they didn't live long enough to crow about it.'

'Well, whatever. He sure didn't pass any horse sense on to his son. That there Grant Hornstone is dumber than a sourdough loaf.'

'You're a yellow dog, Dillon,' the voice from the street was insistent, 'and a four-flushing, cheating coyote. I know you're in there. I give you five minutes to come on out and face me or else I'm coming in the saloon and gut-shoot you.'

'Damnit, time was a fella could enjoy a card game without some loudmouth spoiling it.'

'That ain't no loudmouth, I'm telling you. That's Grant Hornstone. His pa is Sterling Hornstone and like I say he owns the biggest cattle ranch around here.'

'Then why in tarnation's name is he crying about losing a lousy few thousand dollars?'

'The way I heard it, Grant was on his way to Preston to buy cattle for his pa. That money weren't his to gamble with. That money was meant for to buy the cattle.'

'Hell, he's even dumber than I thought. Only a halfwit would behave like that. If his pa is as rich as you say he is, he can stand the loss. It's not my fault his son is a jackass as gambles away his money.'

'Huh! Sterling Hornstone is a hard man. One of the old school. Never gave Grant a kind word. Grant's ma died giving birth to him and the old man blames his son. There's folks reckon he'll take a bullwhip to him from time to time when Grant displeases him. The way I figure it young Hornstone has a choice. If he goes back to the ranch with no cattle and no money then he faces a whipping. So he thinks to call you out and by killing you claim back the money you leave behind in your belongings. It's the only way he escapes a whipping. And he's good with a pistol. He's killed three men already in gunfights. So my advice is to give back the money you won from him and cut your losses. That way you'll live to gamble another day. You go out that door, Hornstone will gun you down and the only thing you'll have won is a plot in boot hill.'

Dexter was staring at the speaker, a look of disbelief on his face.

'What about the law? Ain't there a sheriff in this goddamn town? Surely he don't approve of gunfights?'

The gambler shook his head. 'Bill Purdy only holds his job because Stirling Hornstone hired him. Purdy won't interfere with Grant. Times Grant comes in town, gets liquored up and shoots up the place. Sheriff Purdy stays out of the way till the trouble is over. Grant's so mean he's liable to shoot Purdy just for the hell of it and the sheriff knows it. No one faces up to Grant, not with his quick-fired temper and his old man the most powerful rancher in the district. Stirling Hornstone has enough hands riding for him to come in here and take the whole town apart if he so wished.'

'So what you're saying is, I go out there and get my head shot off or I give this fool his money back.'

'That's the long and short of it. There's no way you're going to win this one. You've been dealt a bum hand. My advice is to fold and cut your losses. That way you just might get out with a whole skin.'

'I ain't sure I like the sound of *might*! What the hell do you mean by that?'

The older man shrugged. 'Even if you give the money back that's no guarantee Grant won't shoot you just for the hell of it. Like I say, he's one mean son of a bitch. No accounting which way he'll jump.'

'I'm coming in, Dillon. An' I'm coming in shooting.'

'Hell, I ain't waiting to be railroaded into a shooting-match with that crazy son of a bitch.'

Dexter Dillon abruptly stood and began scooping dollar bills into his pockets.

'I'm going out the back way. Try and delay that mad cowboy.'

The gambler ran to the rear of the saloon, found the rear door and pushed outside. There was a movement to one side and before he could take evasive action a wooden stake hit him a heavy blow on the side of the head.

'What the. . . .'

Dexter had his gun out and was turning towards his assailant when someone behind clubbed him again. The gambler's legs were buckling but he managed to fire off his gun. There was a scream, then he was hit once more and lights went on and off in his head before darkness closed down.

The four men dragged the limp body of Dexter Dillon down the alley and out behind the livery. The few horses in the corral were the only witnesses as the gang tossed the unconscious gambler to the dirt and spent some minutes rifling his pockets.

'Son of a bitch only got a thousand on him.' Grant Hornstone finished up counting. 'There's two more he took from me. I want that money. The old man will flay the hide off me if I don't get those cattle for him.' As he spoke he kicked the unresponsive body. 'The son of a bitch has gone and lost it all on cards. Hell, what am I going to do?'

'He's maybe hid it somewhere,' suggested one of his companions. 'He ain't likely to carry all that money on him. We ought go back to his room and find it.'

'Jeeze, man, I sure hope so. Maybe we better keep him safe till we find it. When he comes to we'll beat it out of him.' Grant kicked the gambler again. 'Take him in the livery out of sight. I'll go back to the Bottom Dollar and find out what room he's staying in. When we have the money safe we can put a bullet in his head and dump him.'

'Are you sure that's wise, Grant? Folk heard you calling him out. They might just connect you to his killing.'

'Hell, Barney, ain't you got no brains? I was with you fellas all night. We never saw the thieving son of a bitch. Didn't he vamoose out the back door of the Bottom Dollar and we never did catch up on him. We give each other alibis. Anybody got a problem with that?'

Grant glared at his companions. They shuffled uncomfortably, staring at the unconscious gambler or at the horses in the corral, anywhere but look at Hornstone with that mean look in his eyes.

3

Gainsborough had been built in the shape of a T with the top section being Long Street, which ran parallel with the original stage road. There was hope amongst the denizens of the town that the railroad might one day follow the stage line and bring added prosperity to the borough. It was there that the first settlers had built their houses and places of business and it retained its rough image with saloons and gambling halls.

This end of town was relatively quiet during the day, the only activity taking place in the stores and places of business. False fronted stores lined the main road, and trade relating to cattle and farming kept the town moderately busy on most days of the week. However at night and on weekends the streets took on a lively aspect, with cowboys rolling in from the neighbouring ranches to let off steam.

The bottom end of the T contained the newer and more respectable quarters of town. Here dwelt the stolid citizens, where the streets remained quiet at night and on Sunday respectable folk dressed in their best duds and attended church. Gainsborough had the appearance of a prosperous town with a growing population. Dillon pulled up his horse and sat observing the traffic on the streets.

'Sure looks lively enough,' he observed to his horse. 'If Dexter figured to set up in business here I can think of worse places to do so.'

After the initial apprehension of leaving the army, and having spent a couple of weeks on the trail, Dillon was

14

getting to like his newly acquired independence. For years he had been subjected to the discipline of the army. Everything was done in the companionship of his fellow soldiers. They ate together, shared the same hardships and the same dangers. Now for the first time in years Dillon was thrown on his own company and was beginning to like it.

On his journey from the fort to Gainsborough he pitched camp when he liked, bought whatever food supplies that took his fancy and wore civilian duds. He had even packed away his Navy Colt, believing he was finished living with the threat of attack every time he took out a patrol.

Gently he eased his mount along the street looking for the livery. His horse needed a mite of pampering, as did his rider. Dillon was looking forward to meeting his bother and indulging in a spot of drinking and eating something he hadn't cooked himself. At the livery when he paid for a week's board and feed, he asked the attendant where he would find the Bottom Dollar saloon.

'Right the other end of the street from here. You can't miss it. The Bottom Dollar is the big building at the end. If you're looking for rooms and entertaining that's the place. Then there's a boarding house over on Pendle Street that takes in lodgers. If you like a peaceable sleep that'll be the place for you. And good home cooking, too. Annie Grimly feeds her guests real good. You can get a meal there even if you don't take one of her rooms. I'm only telling you that because it tends to get a mite rowdy down at the Dollar, especially at weekends.'

The saloon was moderately busy with a few hardy drinkers at the bar. There was a sprinkling of games in progress at the tables. Dillon bellied up to the bar and ordered a beer.

'I'm looking for Dexter Dillon,' he told the bartender.

It might have been Dillon's imagination but an expression of wariness surfaced for a moment on the man's face.

'Who wants to know?'

The question raised questions of its own in Dillon's mind. He shrugged and picked up his beer.

'Oh, I'm just an old acquaintance of his. He told me once if I was ever down this way I was to look him up. Said as he would buy me a drink.'

The guardedness in the barman's eyes disappeared and he appeared to relax.

'Dexter won't be buying no drinks never again.'

A coldness was creeping into Dillon's gut like when you're out on patrol and you spot Injun sign. The danger was there but you couldn't see it and it made a man wary.

'So what happened? He move on, then?'

'Sure as hell did – moved right into the morgue.'

A cold hand was probing Dillon's chest, making it hard to breathe. He forced himself to remain calm and managed to speak without a tremor.

'The morgue – you mean he's passed on?'

'Afraid so. That's where they put you when you're dead.'

Dillon wanted to reach over, grab the tender by the shirt and yank him across the counter.

'Sad,' he said, holding in his anger. 'Must have been sudden. The Dexter I knew was only a young fella. He had years of living ahead of him.'

'Not with a piece of lead in his head.'

In spite of the sick feeling inside Dillon tried to feign nonchalance, asking the obvious question. 'How'd it happen?'

'Nobody knows. Found him stretched out behind the livery.'

'How long ago was this?'

'Day afore yesterday.'

'You say he's in the morgue?'

'Last I heard.'

Dillon picked up his beer and drained it. 'Guess I'd better mosey on down there and pay my respects. Is there a sheriff's office in town?'

'Sheriff Bill Purdy. The jail is on the far side of the street about halfway along. Can't miss it. There's a sign outside reads Sheriff's Office.'

The barkeep sniggered when he imparted this information and again Dillon had to restrain himself from reaching over and grabbing the man; instead he swung on his heel and left the saloon.

'You a relative?'

The undertaker was a chubby, cheerful individual, not at all how Dillon imagined a man in the undertaking profession would look.

'Friend.' Dillon's answer was terse.

His nerves were all jumpy inside and he wanted to bawl. It was with great trepidation that he waited to see the body he believed to be his brother, but hoping some terrible misunderstanding had taken place. On his walk along the street towards the morgue he had convinced himself it was all a big mistake. He would find the body was that of some stranger – not Dexter.

'Has anyone identified him?'

'Sure thing. Everyone knew Mr Dillon. Quiet, well-behaved and kept himself respectable. Though he did gamble a lot. I reckon that's what got him killed. Rumour has it he won a big pot from. . . .' Suddenly the man ceased speaking as if he had said enough. 'This way.'

Before Dillon could put further questions to the man,

he was led into a back room with a row of trestles along one wall. On three of these rested sheeted figures. When the undertaker pulled the sheet back Dillon's knees went weak. He reached out and held on to the table to steady himself.

'You all right, mister. . . ? Sorry, I didn't catch your name.'

'O'Grady.' Dillon said the first name that came into his head.He didn't know why, but he wanted to keep his identity secret for the time being. Some instinct had been wakened in him. It was the way the barkeep had behaved and now the undertaker had stopped telling him something that might explain why Dexter was killed.

'You seem a mite distressed.'

'I'll be OK. Just ain't used to seeing dead bodies close up like this.'

Which was a lie seeing as during his soldering days Dillon had seen plenty of dead, both friend and foe, and had frequently added to the tally himself. Something he did not like to dwell on. For long moments he stared at the battered features of his dead brother. Slowly he drew the sheet further down seeing bruises on the body. There was no sign of a gunshot wound.

'He's been beaten. Barkeep said he was shot.'

'He got it in the back of the skull.'

'Can I see?'

'Listen, Mr O'Grady, I can't go manhandling corpses about for any old stranger that comes in out of nowhere.'

Dillon reached out and took his brother by the shoulder and raised the body. He almost broke down then as he felt the coldness of the dead flesh.

'Mr O'Grady, I must insist.'

Dillon ignored the undertaker's protests. He studied the bullet wound for a few moments then gently let the body rest back on the table.

'When's the funeral?'

'Day after tomorrow. Will you be attending?'

'Yes, I figure it's the least I can do.'

Without another word Dillon turned and walked from the morgue.

4

Sheriff Purdy was a middle-aged ex-cowpoke. He had worked as ramrod for Stirling Hornstone for a good many years when an accident left him with a stiff leg and unfit for the rigorous duties of running the vast Hornstone cattle ranch. Rather than throw his employee on the scrapheap Hornstone had shoehorned him into the job of law officer. A smart arrangement as it gave him another hold on the institutions of Ruffin County.

Hornstone had tentacles in almost every aspect of commerce in the area. He already owned the bank and the general store and the Hornstone ranch was the biggest spread for miles. The rancher boasted to his friends he could start at one boundary in the morning and it would take him till the afternoon to reach the furthest.

When Dillon stepped into the sheriff's office he found a fresh-faced man with a mop of grey hair. Sheriff Purdy looked up, nodded at his visitor, removed his reading glasses and placed them on top of the newspaper spread on his desk.

'Howdy, Sheriff Bill Purdy at your service. What can I do for you?'

'Howdy. I'm just passing through and thought to look up an old friend of mine. Fella name of Dexter Dillon. Someone informs me he was shot a few nights ago. Maybe you can tell me what happened?'

'Yeah, sad case. Nice young fella, real friendly.' The sheriff shook his head forlornly. 'The livery man found the body Tuesday morning lying out the back of the stables.'

'You found the killer, yet?'

'Nah, and we got nothing to go on neither. Nobody knows a thing about it. Mind you, it is early days yet.'

'You have been investigating the murder, Sheriff? Somebody must know something. Like heard the gunshot or seen who was about at the time of the killing.'

'What did you say your name was?' The sheriff was frowning at his visitor.

'I didn't say, but it's Michael O'Grady.'

'You say you're a friend of the deceased?'

'Well, more acquaintance than friend. He told me he was thinking of opening a saloon and told me to look him up if I was ever down this way. I guess he won't be opening no saloon now.'

'The only thing he'll be opening is a hole in boot hill. Sorry I can't help you more, Mr O'Grady.'

Sheriff Purdy replaced his glasses on his nose and went back to reading, indicating the interview was at an end. Dillon stared at the mop of grey hair bent over the paper, doing his best to damp down the anger building up inside him. His brother murdered and it looked like the local law wasn't too bothered about finding the killer. Realizing he would get nothing further from the sheriff, Dillon left the law office.

On his way back to the Bottom Dollar saloon Dillon

decided to play it cool and not make it too obvious he was interested in the killing of his brother. There was something odd about the way people were so cagey when he asked questions about the murder. A more cunning strategy was called for if he was to get to the bottom of this mystery. Gambling – that was Dexter's favourite pastime and it seemed to be connected in some way with the killing. Dillon decided it was in that activity where he might find out more.

Back at the saloon he booked a room for the week and, as the evening settled in, so he was idling about the gaming-tables watching the activity. Inevitably someone noticed him hanging about and invited him to join them.

'Howdy, stranger, you looking to have a game?'

'Don't mind if I do, long as I can afford the stakes.'

'Ah, we have our moments. Would have frightened your purse back into your pocket the other night when big money exchanged hands.'

'That so. What do you call big money around here?'

'At one stage there was five grand in the kitty. Makes a fella's eyes water just to think on it.'

Dillon whistled. 'Five big ones, you say? That's well out of my league. Who pocketed the jackpot?'

The man scowled. 'Poor fella didn't live long to spend his winnings. He was shot dead the next night.'

'Holy smoke! The fella he won from must have been a poor loser.'

The card player glanced uneasily around at his companions. 'No, no, it weren't nothing like that.' Then, abruptly changing the subject, 'Are you staying in or raising the bet?'

'I raise you two dollars.'

During the course of the game Dillon gently probed for

information about the card game that had ended so tragically for his brother. For he was in no doubt it had been Dexter who had been the winner of the big money and that that could have been the direct cause of his death. But no matter how subtle he was the gamblers would not be drawn, and he soon realized no one was willing to discuss the happenings of a few nights ago.

Recognizing he would gain nothing from continuing the game Dillon folded after losing about twenty dollars, but he felt it was money well spent. From what little had been said he knew he had to find out more about that card game – who the participants were and who had been the biggest losers. He was certain the men he had played with tonight had suddenly clammed up because they were afraid of saying too much. That game and subsequent events held the clue to the reason for someone beating and shooting Dexter, and whoever was responsible was someone to be feared. But then that was obvious, for that person had killed already.

Dillon drifted to the bar and ordered a whiskey. He stood sipping it while he mulled over his next move. The town drunk, seeing the stranger at the bar, decided to put the bite on him, on the off-chance that he might be an easy mark.

'Howdy fella. You're not from around these parts.'

Dillon could smell the stale alcohol on the man, both on his breath and on his clothes.

'That's right, just passing through.'

The man began patting his pockets as if looking for something.

'Ain't that a dang thing? Must have left my money in my other clothes.' The souse looked wistfully at his mark. 'Don't suppose you could lend a fella a dollar to buy a drink? Save me going all the way home again.'

The barkeep had moved up to them on the other side of the counter. 'Joe, leave the man alone. He don't want no stinking drunk breathing in his air.'

'Humph, you wouldn't have spoken like that to me when I was in the United States cavalry. I'd'a pitted you on the end of my blade like a mangy apple. Goddamn no respect you haven't. I fought for my country which is more than what you ever did. All you know is pouring drinks and insulting people. One of these days when I find my bayonet I'll come in here and stick it up your mangy ass. That ought to sharpen you up, you ornery cuss.'

Dillon was amused as he saw the barkeep, an over-weight, bald man grow red in the face.

'That's it!' he roared. 'Out, afore I throw you out.'

'Huh, it'll take a man to do that, Harry Waters. And you ain't no man – you're a fat tub of blubber.'

Suddenly the barkeep produced a truncheon from beneath the counter and swung it at the old man. The baton was thick polished wood and if it had landed might have cracked Joe's head open. It never got there for a hand came over and caught the club as it descended.

'Goddamn it, what you playing at, fella?'

The enraged barkeep tried to recover his club, but Dillon kept his grip, easily retaining it as the beefy barman struggled against him.

'Ain't no call to go beating up on this gent just because he slung a few home truths at you.'

The barman glared at Dillon while he yanked in vain at the club. For all the give in the stranger's grip he might as well have been trying to move the bar behind which he served.

'Mister, I'm barring you as well as this old coot. And that room you booked I let to someone else.'

Dillon gave a sudden twist while at the same time

chopping the edge of his hand into the man's bicep. The barman gave a yelp and let go his weapon. Suddenly he found himself yanked across the top of his own bar with his baton wedged underneath his chin.

'Mister, you'll refund the money I left as a deposit for my lodgings and to make up for the inconvenience you'll donate a bottle of bourbon. Else this baton might just find its way into the place where this old man wanted to put his bayonet.'

The barkeep saw something in his opponent's eyes that scared the hell out of him. He nodded.

'OK, OK, no need to get riled up. I was only funning.'

'Just do as I say, and don't forget the bottle.'

5

Dillon's companion could not stop chuckling as he sucked at the bottle of bourbon that had come unexpectedly into his possession.

'He, he, he, he. Goddamn it, I ain't seen nothing like it in a coon's age. I always suspected Harry Waters were a yellow-bellied coward. When you took his bat away and shoved it in his face, he must have filled his pants. He, he, he, he.'

Dillon smiled indulgently as the old man rattled on and chuckled and drank the bourbon. They were in Joe's shack, a ramshackle abode that looked as if a good wind would reduce it to a pile of kindling. A candle guttered in a tin saucer, dimly illuminating the interior which was maybe just as well for the shack appeared to be filled with a clutter of rubbish.

Dillon knew he would have to go and find the boarding house in Pendle Street that the livery hand had told him about if he wanted a bed for the night. The incident with the surly barkeep had put paid to his room in the Bottom Dollar. But for now he had an ulterior motive for accepting the old man's hospitality.

Joe might be a drunk but he seemed to have all his wits about him and Dillon was hoping he might reveal something about the circumstances leading up to his brother's murder. So he stayed on and let the man drink the bourbon, thinking it might loosen his tongue enough to reveal what he knew about the killing. Dillon reckoned he had to tread warily, for up to now everyone clammed up when the night in question surfaced in conversation.

'You ever play cards, Joe?'

'Hell no, I ain't got the money to waste on such things. The mean bastards round here won't extend a man's credit. Old man Hornstone owns the bank. They hold on to the money tighter than a preacher clasps his Bible and with even less charity.'

'Hornstone – he the banker then?'

'Hornstone ain't no banker – he's God.'

'God! Sort of fella you bow down to and worship?'

'If you want to be anything in this town you got to do just that. He owns the whole goddamn town.'

'A baron then, like in medieval times.'

'Don't know about no baron but he's sure one mean bastard.'

Dillon was trying to measure the level in the bottle. He didn't want his companion to pass out before he could pump him for information. But it was difficult to see in the dim light, so he decided he'd better press on before his host emptied the bottle and was rendered incapable of rational conversation.

'If he owns the bank then he would have handled the money that fella won in the big card game the other night.'

'That money never went in no bank.'

Joe took another swig from the bottle. Dillon waited, hoping the man would elaborate.

'No siree. That's where all the trouble started. Hornstone lost that money. It weren't his to lose. No siree. It weren't his to lose.'

'What, the banker was playing cards with someone else's money? Weren't that a mite risky?'

'No, no, no, no, no! It were Grant as were playing with Stirling's money.'

'Grant – he the bank clerk, then?'

'Nah, Grant is Stirling Hornstone's son. You see, Grant was to buy cattle for his pa with the money but Grant sat in a poker game and lost the lot. The fella as got killed – young Dillon – he won it all. Well, that made Grant mad. He claimed as Dillon cheated. He claimed he'd kill the son of a bitch if he didn't pay it back.'

The bottle tipped up and the glug-glug of liquid going down the old man's gullet was plain to hear in the silence of the shack. Dillon's insides were cold as he listened to the tale. Dexter winning a big pot of money from the banker's son and the banker's brat ratting on the bet and demanding his money back. And Dexter being Dexter wouldn't do it. So they killed him.

Dillon's head was reeling as he took it all in. If the town drunk knew all this then why hadn't the people he had spoken to not given him the information? The liveryman had been evasive. The undertaker and the gamblers would not talk about it. But the worst feature was the attitude of the sheriff. The man claimed no one knew a thing about the killing, yet this old drunk could put it all together. Was the sheriff that dumb or was there some other reason for feigning ignorance about the crime?

But in one way it made sense. As Joe told it, Hornstone had such a powerful hold on the territory that folk would be scared to cross him. Would that fear overcome their scruples to such an extent that they would cover up for murder? Surely a community couldn't be that corrupt.

'Hell, I been a soldier so long I don't know how civilized folk behave,' Dillon muttered. 'Maybe it's like the army and everyone covers up for everyone else.'

'You're not drinking, my friend,' Joe said, slurring his words while at the same time clutching the precious bottle to his chest. 'Likker is the only stuff that makes sense in this goddamn world. I reckon it was the Good Lord hisself as formenticated likker. You take a few slugs of this.' He patted the bottle. 'An' the world begins to mellow. A few more swallows an' you start to tolerate fellas as you can't usually stand the sight of. Let me tell you this, friend . . . I keep callin' you friend. Wass your name anyway?'

Lost in his speculation of the circumstances that led up to Dexter's death Dillon answered absent-mindedly.

'Captain Tim Dillon, Fifteenth Cavalry division.'

'Consarn it, I knew it. You a cavalry man like me. We attract each other like maggots. Thass what we do. Joe Briggs of the Thirty Fourth. Man, did we give those Rebels a bloody nose at Fisher's Hill. "Give them the steel," cried Colonel Bridgewater. We rode at them like demons – like demons we were. Went through their ranks like a rampaging herd of bulls we did, flourishing our sabres. Slash to the right – hack to the left. A lot of blood spilled that day. My blade was blunt by the time we hauled rein and turned to give it another go. But they broke then. Couldn't take no more. Colonel got a medal for that day's work. It was us as did the cutting and him as got the medal. I was so proud that day.' The bottle tilted and Joe swallowed noisily. 'Goddamn bottle's empty. You could have left me a drop.'

Dillon watched the bottle slide to the floor and Joe's head tilted forward.

'Gave 'em hell that day,' he mumbled. 'Gave 'em hell. . . .'

Dillon got hold of the old fella and manhandled him over to the corner of the room to a bed that was nothing but a pile of old blankets and unwashed garments. He stood looking down at the snoring man, but he wasn't seeing an old drunk; he was seeing instead the battered body of his brother stretched out on a slab in the morgue.

6

In spite of the lateness of the hour there was a light on in the boarding house. When Dillon knocked the door was opened and a middle-aged female with grey hair tied up in a bun and wearing an apron answered the door.

'Ma'am, I apologize for calling at this time of the night but I'm in need of a room.'

'Come in.'

The woman turned and walked back inside, leaving Dillon to close the door and follow her into a room furnished with cotton-covered tables and lattice-backed chairs. She lit a lamp on a mantel and when it was glowing to her satisfaction turned and studied her guest.

'You must be the fella as was thrown out of the Bottom Dollar.'

Dillon raised his eyebrows, wondering how she knew about that. It was less than a couple of hours ago it had happened.

'Yes, ma'am, but I ain't a troublemaker. I promise I won't cause you any bother.'

'The last fella caused me trouble got a bad dose of the runs after I fixed his food for him. Must have spent a whole two days on the john. Time he crawled back in here he was so weak I was able to take him by the scruff of the neck and sling him out on his ass. Never had no more bother since.'

'I could see how as that would drag the stuffing out of a fella. I sure wouldn't want to rub you up the wrong way, ma'am.'

She glared back at him. 'Heard you stood up for Joe Briggs; saved him a broken head as it were told me. Must be some good in a man as stood up for an old soak like Joe. You hungry?'

'Now you mention it, ma'am, I am a mite.'

'Set you down there. I got some mutton stew if that's all right with you.'

A wave of weariness swept over Dillon as he slumped into a chair.

'How the hell does she know about me and Joe?' he muttered. 'The gossip gang sure operates efficiently in this here burg.'

In view of the excellence of the hole-and-corner activities operating in the town Dillon speculated on the reticence of the citizens to reveal anything about Dexter's killing.

This Hornstone got such a grip on the territory everyone is scared to speak out against him. It's worrisome to think that one man could have such a hold on a community. There's only two ways to have such power – fear or respect. And I suspect the former. Else why would folk cover up for a murderer?

His mutton stew arrived accompanied by a hunk of bread. Dillon fell to and shovelled the food in. While he was eating his hostess brought in two mugs of coffee and sat at the table with him.

'How long you need the room? Dollar a day with food. No spitting, no females, no fighting, no cussing, no blasphemy, no Injuns.'

'I ain't figuring on doing any of them things, ma'am. I need the room for a week. I can pay in advance. Can I ask you a few questions?'

'Fire away.'

'How come you know what happened with Joe in the saloon?'

'Not much goes on in this town I don't get to know about sooner or later.'

'So not many secrets, then?'

'I sure as shooting hope not.'

'There's a dead man in the morgue, name of Dexter Dillon. Who killed him?'

'You finished that stew? I'll take the dish. Then I'll show you to your room.'

At that point Dillon knew for certain that the men or man responsible for murdering Dexter were part of the Hornstone empire, and the finger of suspicion pointed at Grant Hornstone, the son of Stirling Hornstone.

When Dillon fell into bed he did not sleep but tossed and turned, his mind spinning unceasingly in a dizzying vortex of anger and frustration. Towards dawn he fell into a fitful sleep, his mind tortured by images of his brother. Sometimes Dexter sat up and asked Tim who killed him.

At one stage the spectre accused Tim of the killing.

In the morning, lying awake, his eyes gritty from lack of sleep, Dillon had decided on his course of action. He planned to confront the sheriff and see how far the plot to cover up for the killers of Dexter would go.

Breakfast over, he walked to the livery to see his horse, then made his way along the street to the saloon. The barkeep scowled at him but stayed quiet.

'I come to collect my things.'

'They're out back. I had to clear the room.'

There was a malicious gleam in the man's eyes, which warned Dillon.

'Anything damaged, I'll come looking for reparation.'

'Just get your stuff and get out of my saloon,' the big man snarled. 'You're not welcome in here no more. This town don't like troublemakers.'

When the barkeep said his things were out back he meant in the yard. Dillon stood staring at his belongings scattered carelessly for anyone to rummage through. His rage boiled over and he turned and went back inside.

'You thieving son of a bitch. You've messed me about for the last time.'

Then he stopped. Anticipating his return the barkeep had a twelve gauge resting on the counter, pointing directly at Dillon.

'Mister, you want a bellyful of lead shot you keep on coming. I'll be within my rights to blow you to kingdom come. I already told you you ain't welcome here. My advice is to get on your horse, ride out of this town and keep on going.'

His rage boiling over, Dillon realized it was stalemate. Abruptly he swung around and went back to gather his possessions. He saw with some dismay that his identity and discharge papers had been rifled. Now everyone knew who he was and why he was so interested in finding out who had killed Dexter.

He deposited his kit in the livery stable, telling the owner he would collect them later, and made his way along to the sheriff's office. This time there was no friendly greeting when he went inside. Instead the sheriff stared at him with active hostility.

'Mister, you been making a public nuisance of yourself. I've had a complaint from Harry Waters at the Bottom Dollar that you attacked him. You also come in here, giving a false name, trying to pry into a killing that has all the marks of a straightforward robbery. I could throw you in the jug for any of those misdemeanours. So from now on keep your nose clean. My advice is to bury your brother and ride on back to where you came from.'

'I never told you who I was because everyone I spoke to about my brother's murder clammed up tight. It was as if everyone was trying to cover up for the killer. And that includes you, Sheriff.'

'You son of a bitch, who're you accusing? I could lock you up for any of those offences. Nobody knows who killed your brother. We're doing all we can to find him. Without witnesses it'll take a while to solve. Maybe someone will remember something that will help. But until that happens you keep yourself to yourself and don't go poking your nose into things you know nothing about.'

'Does the name Grant Hornstone mean anything to you?'

The lawman's jaw tightened and some colour crept in his face.

'Sure it means something. Everyone knows his pa owns the Hornstone ranch. What the hell that got to do with anything?'

'The story is Dexter won a pile of money from this

Hornstone. Next thing my brother is beaten up and then shot. My guess is the man he won the money from came looking for it and when he couldn't find it he battered Dexter to find out where the money was. Then to cover up he shot him. The man all this points to is this Grant Hornstone.'

The sheriff was leaning back in his chair, shaking his head.

'You're one crazy son of a bitch. Grant Hornstone is the son of the richest man in the area. Stirling Hornstone owns the biggest spread, he owns the bank and he don't need to go round killing and robbing. If you go about spreading those rumours Hornstone will come after you and sue your ass off. Someone knew your brother had that money and went after it and it weren't no goddamn rancher's son. Haven't you suffered enough, losing your brother? Do you want to lose your liberty also? For sure as hell if you go around slinging accusations like that and Hornstone gets to hear he won't rest till he has you run out of the county or put behind bars. My advice is to bury your brother, ride on out of Gainsborough and let the law find his killer.'

'Why is everyone so anxious for me to ride on out of Gainsborough?'

7

Amelia Huger tightened the braces on the harness, then stepped back to examine her work. The ancient mule regarded her sombrely.

'Pickaxe, I know you like to loaf around the farm and eat your damn fool head off, but like it or not, today we are going to town.' She turned her attention to the vehicle. 'I ain't sure which is the more prehistoric, this wagon or my aged mule.'

She spent a few moments critically examining the vehicle – tugging at the wheels, feeling over the shafts, till eventually she stood back, hands on hips, pursed her lips and then sighed.

'I guess it will carry us into town and back again.' Turning she trudged across to the small neatly built ranch house. 'Raoul,' she called out, 'are you ready yet? You know what day it is?'

Her ten-year-old son appeared in the doorway, pulling his fingers through his tousled hair, trying to smooth it into some semblance of order.

'Sure, Ma, I know. We're going into Gainsborough for Dad.'

'I got the wagon hitched up. Just a couple more things and then we're ready.'

Amelia disappeared inside and moments later reappeared carrying a rifle, a bunch of flowers and a small pot of paint. She pulled the door to and went over to the wagon, where her son was already aboard.

'Can I drive, Ma?'

'Sure.' Amelia wedged the rifle against the seat and placed the flowers and paint on the floor between herself and her son. 'But if Pickaxe gets spooked and breaks into a wild gallop, you think you can handle him?'

It was an old joke. The mule had one speed and nothing would shift him beyond the unhurried steady amble that would eventually get them to Gainsborough.

'Hee-haw!' Raoul yelled and flicked the reins. 'Pickaxe,

I want you to lift up them hoofs and shake off the dust of this here place. I've entered you for the Kentucky Derby and I want you to show me a burst of speed that'll leave all them there thoroughbreds behind.'

The mule leaned into the traces and, creaking and rattling, the ancient rig moved slowly out of the yard. Amelia smiled fondly as her son grinned at her, pleased with his funning.

'One day Pickaxe will take you seriously and do just that.'

'Wouldn't that be something?'

Upon arriving in Gainsborough the boy drove the wagon through the streets and turned up towards the older part of town. They pulled up at the cemetery gates and Amelia stared across at the solitary figure standing inside. Solemnly mother and son dismounted and, carrying the flowers in one hand and her son's hand in the other, she walked into the graveyard. The man inside did not look up and Amelia was able to study him.

She saw a tall, rangy man dressed in buckskins moodily contemplating a newly dug grave. He was obviously sunk in grief and stood bareheaded, holding his hat in hands folded across his belt. The man was clean-shaven, with dark hair cropped short. He took no notice of the newcomers as they entered.

They passed the lone mourner and reached their destination. Amelia handed the flowers to Raoul, then bent and cleared old faded blooms from the grave. She nodded to Raoul and he placed the flowers on the grave. Together they knelt and bowed their heads.

'Please God, take care of Pa. I miss him and so does Ma. I wish you hadn't let him be killed like you did but then maybe you were too busy that day.'

Amelia couldn't help the tears. She thought that by

now there would be no tears to shed. Raoul squeezed her hand.

The inscription on the headboard read: In loving memory of Edward Huger 1855-1883. Someone had gone to the bother of painting over the rest of the inscription. Amelia opened the paintpot and with a small brush did some lettering on top of the blanked-out section.

'Murdered by Grant Hornstone and Sheriff Purdy.' She murmured the words as she painted.

Every month the little family visited the grave and each time found the original inscription obliterated. Amelia would repaint the accusation that her husband was murdered and naming his killers. Her task complete, Amelia and her son stood in quiet contemplation for a few more moments.

'They'll do it every time, Ma. Why do you still write it on?'

'Your pa was a good man. I know he won't get justice in this world, so each time I write that on Pa's tomb I'm hoping someone up there will pay attention and one day do something about it.'

They stood a moment or two more.

'Let's go, son.'

When they turned from the grave the solitary mourner was still there in exactly the same stance. Amelia wondered who was buried there that held the man's attention. She supposed it must have been his wife and felt a twinge of sympathy for the man. He was a stranger to her, but then she did not know everyone in Gainsborough for no one wanted to socialize with someone who defied the powerful Hornstones for fear of being indicted along with her. Amelia noticed that the new grave was bare of any decoration and on impulse she bent and extracted some blossoms from her own bunch.

'Sorry if I disturb you, mister. I thought maybe you

might like these few flowers for your grave?'

Grey eyes filled with anguish gazed at her and for a moment Amelia forgot her own grief. He stared for so long that Amelia though he was going to ignore her offer, but then he reached out.

'Thank you, ma'am.'

For no reason she could think of Amelia blushed deeply. To cover her confusion she looked at the board on the grave.

'Dexter Dillon,' she read out. 'Was he a friend?'

The stranger bent and placed the flowers on the bare earth.

'My brother.'

'Oh, I'm so sorry. You probably want to be alone just now.'

'I am alone. No one in this town wants to talk to me. No one wants to be seen talking to me. For your own good, ma'am, if I was you, I'd leave now. It won't do your reputation no good to be seen associating with a pariah.'

It was her turn to gaze steadily back at him.

'Mr Dillon, I don't give a gnat's foreleg what the people in this town think. I am not welcome in this town neither. I shall go down there to the store to buy a few essentials afore setting back home. Mr Blakemore, who runs the store, will refuse to serve me. I have to loiter inside, getting in his way. I stand in front of any display I think his customers are interested in and mess with them. Some folk, when they see me in there, turn around and walk back out again. In the end Blakemore has to serve me just to get rid of me.'

He was frowning at her. 'Do you owe him money?'

'I get no credit in this town. I have to pay for everything up front in hard cash. Come, Raoul, let's leave Mr Dillon in peace. Good day.'

Dillon watched the couple walk back to the mule-drawn wagon. When they were gone he went across to the grave with the fresh flowers. For long moments he studied the headboard and the newly painted letters.

8

It happened just as she had told the stranger. Blakemore, who ran the store for Stirling Hornstone, feigned indifference to her requests.

'I'm busy at the moment. You'll have to wait.'

So she waited, damping down her anger. If she allowed her resentment to fire up there was no knowing what she might do. It was what they wanted. They were hoping she would crack and do something outrageous so they could haul her up in court and send her to prison or impose a crippling fine. Amelia always made Raoul stay out in the wagon during these embarrassing episodes, not wanting him to witness her humiliation.

The store emptied and still Blakemore did not approach her, which was to be expected. He would draw out the process as long as he dared until he tired of the game, then he would serve her, sneering all the while and asking if she was sure she could afford the goods.

As she dawdled about, picking up items on display and replacing them in different positions, she wondered how the stout storekeeper would react if she went back out and brought her carbine and threatened to shoot him if he did not serve her. The idea brought a bitter smile to her lips.

Two women entered, looked disdainfully at Amelia before walking to the counter. Impulsively she reached out and knocked over a cylindrical container of walking sticks. The resulting noise created by the cascading articles was rewardingly alarming.

'Oh, dear,' she exclaimed, smiling brightly at the two women, at the same time noting how red the storekeeper's face had became. 'How clumsy of me.'

For the next few minutes she enjoyed herself making as much racket as she could, picking up the spilled sticks and tossing them one by one back into the container.

Her thoughts strayed to the stranger in the cemetery and she wondered what crime he had committed to place him on the town's blacklist. It was as if her thought had summoned him, for at that moment he wandered into the store. Amelia smiled a greeting but he looked through her.

So much for doing a person a good turn, she thought bitterly. It seemed there were no decent men left in the world. Not since her own dear Edward had been taken from her. The world was filled with stupid, selfish, sheep-like people who danced to whatever tune Stirling Hornstone whistled.

'Good day, sir. Be with you in a moment.' Blakemore escorted his female customers to the door, then turned back to the stranger. 'Can I help you?'

'Yeah, I need some supplies.' There was a pause. 'Perhaps you should serve that young lady. She was here before me.'

Amelia tensed and dared not look up.

'That's all right, sir, she can wait.'

'Oh no, I insist. Serve that lady while I think on what I need.'

But Blakemore was not to be moved. 'The woman is a timewaster. I said she can wait.'

'Oh, very well. I need flour, molasses, bacon. . . .'

Amelia, disappointed that Mr Dillon had given in so

easily, listened to his requirements and wished she had the money to order such a lavish amount of goods.

'How much candy?'

'I'll have the whole jar.'

Blakemore was having a great time putting up the order. Every now and then he would smirk across at Amelia.

'That'll be twenty dollars fifteen cents.'

'How's about we settle for the even twenty dollars.'

'Certainly, sir. I never mind giving discount to a good paying customer.'

Tim counted out the money.

'Where would you like this delivered, sir?'

'There's a wagon right outside – just pile it all in there.'

'Yes, sir, I can do that.'

Blakemore carried a heaped box to the door, where he hesitated. 'Where is the wagon? I don't see any.'

Dillon was right behind him, carrying the rest of the order in a sack.

'You'll be needing a new pair of specs. It's right in front of your nose.'

'There must be some mistake. That wagon belongs to Mrs Huger.'

'Bless my soul, so it does. Well, put it in there anyway. I'm sure she won't mind.'

Dillon turned and smiled at Amelia. Her mouth was gaping open and she was staring at him in bewilderment.

'Hurry up, man. I'm sure the lady wants to get on home afore dark sets in.'

Dillon nudged the storekeeper with the bulging sack, forcing him through the door. Blakemore had no option. Glowering, he slid the box of goods into the wagon with Dillon following and heaving the sack of groceries in with it.

Dillon retrieved the jar of candies and walking round to the front of the wagon handed it to a bemused Raoul.

'You like candies, son?'

'Sure thing, mister.' Clutching the jar the youngster hesitated. 'This don't seem right. We never buy candy.'

By this time Amelia had overcome her surprise and was outside.

'What's going on?' She was staring in consternation at the loaded wagon. 'We can't afford all this.'

Dillon swept off his hat. 'Ma'am, I was grieving alone for my dead brother when a kindly stranger thought to hand me flowers for his grave. These measly supplies are not enough to repay the gift of compassion that brought me some comfort in my sorrow.'

She stared back at him and unaccountably tears sprang into her eyes.

'There was no need,' she whispered. 'I . . .' but she couldn't trust herself to speak any more. She was afraid she would break down before Blakemore.

'Thank you.'

In a daze she climbed up beside Raoul, who was unable to say anything for his mouth was stuffed with candy. She took up the reins and flicked them across the mule's withers.

Dillon stood in the street watching the wagon recede into the distance.

'Mister, you don't know what you've done – giving stuff to that woman. She's a troublemaker and sure as there's a God in heaven, she'll bring down trouble on you if you let her.'

Dillon did not deign to reply. He started down the street in the direction of the livery. Today he had buried his brother. Now it was time to confront the man who murdered him.

9

Dillon could see the huge iron sign rearing into the air long before he was close enough to decipher it. His guess as to what it was proved correct. The iron letters: HORN-STONE told the world who ruled here. Mounted men carrying carbines patrolled the barbed wire fence and he was stopped at the gate under the sign by a bearded lookout.

'Where you headed, stranger?'

'I'm here to see Mr Hornstone.'

'What's your business with him?'

'I come to see if he's hiring.'

'We ain't hiring at this time.'

'Ain't that for him to decide?'

The guard shrugged. 'Just trying to save you a mite of time, fella.'

The gate was tugged open enough for Dillon to ride through.

What looked like a small village spread out from the stone-built ranch house. Bunkhouses and barns and silos and corrals sprawled out into the grassland. Cowboys worked with horses and cattle. Somewhere in the clatter of human and animal activities could be heard the sound of iron on iron as a blacksmith worked at an anvil. Two armed guards stopped Dillon before he got to the house.

'What you want?'

'I came to see Mr Hornstone. This is his place, ain't it?'

'What's it about?' Ignoring the sarcasm in Dillon's question.

'It's about my brother.'

'What about your brother – does he work here?'

'No, he was murdered by Hornstone's son.'

'Mister, I'm giving you a piece of friendly advice. Turn your horse around, ride on back to wherever you came from and I'll forget what you just said.'

'Can't do that.'

For long moments the man gazed steadily at Dillon before speaking again. 'I heard it said as some fellas have a death wish. I never thought much to it till now. You push this and you'll more than likely join your brother.' When Dillon did not reply the guard gestured. 'Get down off that nag and wait.'

They walked back up to the house and Dillon saw the guard talking to someone inside. Eventually he strolled back to where Dillon waited.

'Shuck your guns.'

Dillon held his arms out. 'I ain't carrying.'

'Pete, frisk him.'

Dillon stood immobile while he was patted down for weapons.

'Nothing; not even a knife.'

'Walk ahead.'

Dillon studied the man standing on the veranda. He saw a square-faced man wearing a black Stetson. A luxurious moustache covered his upper lip.

'Mister, you got one chance to state your business.' The voice was clipped and authoritative, not unlike those of some senior officers under whom Dillon had once served.

'My brother Dexter Dillon was murdered a few days ago. He won a big pot of money from your son in a poker game. It's my belief your son killed Dexter to get back the money.'

Stirling Hornstone gazed out at the man before him who was making these outrageous accusations.

'Mister, you come in my town, come on my land, ride out to my home and tell lies about my family. You're a stranger here so I'm going to go easy on you. Instead of a hanging you'll get a whipping.'

Then he was gone, a servant opening and shutting the door for him.

Dillon stared at the closed door. He was aware of men closing in on him. He whirled as they came at him, punching a bearded face, dodging a swinging fist and striking hard into a gut, hearing the whoosh of air as the man went down. He shoulder-charged another but a foot hooked out and tripped him. As he went down he grabbed a boot raised to kick him and twisted. There was a yell of agony and a thud as the man hit the dirt. A boot thumped into the side of his head. Then they were crowding around kicking as he struggled to get to his feet. Blows rained down as the cowboys yelled and kicked. A lariat was dropped over his neck and he was hauled gasping and choking to his feet.

Hollering and whooping the crowd of excited cowboys dragged him to a corral and roped him to the rails. The beating had dazed him and he could put up little resistance. Someone produced a knife and his shirt was sliced away.

When the first cut of the whip slashed across his back he almost cried out. After that he gritted his teeth, then lost consciousness as the pain of the flogging grew too agonizing to bear.

They tied him to his horse with the same lariat that had secured him to the fence. Dillon was not aware of passing beneath the iron Hornstone sign when they led his horse out. Someone whacked the beast across the rump and sent it running back to Gainsborough.

Captain Dillon's horse, Monday, so called because that was the day he was issued with the mount, stood in the street with the bloodied body of the ex-soldier in its back. Dillon was fastened securely to the mount with the lariat wound around his body and underneath the horse. No one approached the horse and its gruesome burden.

Once he had learned the identity of the newcomer from the barkeep who had rummaged through Dillon's belongings, Sheriff Purdy had sent a messenger out to Hornstone to warn him of the potential troublemaker. The word came back. Anyone helping Dillon would face severe consequences. So Monday stood fidgeting and restive, sensing that something was badly wrong but unable to do anything about it. That was until Joe, the drunken bum whom Dillon had befriended, came shuffling down the boardwalk wondering how he was going to cadge enough money to buy a drink.

'Consarn my soul, what in tarnation is that?'

Warily he approached and Monday nervously backed away.

'Whoa there, old hoss.' Joe reached out and took hold of the bridle. 'I ain't going to hurt you none.'

It was then Joe noticed the blood and began to take in the condition of the man on the back of the horse.

'Holy slithering sidewinders, it's that fella Dillon, as bought me the bourbon. Aw, what have they done to you, fella?'

Sheriff Purdy was lounging in his office when Joe burst in.

'Sheriff, you got to come. That fella Dillon is out in the street, his back ripped to shreds and tied to his hoss. You got to come and help.'

'Joe, you take my advice and leave well enough alone. Go on back to your kennel and crawl in there till this blows over.'

'What the hell are you blathering on about? That fella out there will die if he don't get help. You got to come and give me a hand with him.'

'I ain't got to do nothing. Don't you know what I'm saying? Word is anyone assists Dillon will have to answer to Hornstone.'

'So that's what this is all about. Dillon poking into his brother's murder. Now Hornstone has him half-killed and we help finish him off.'

'Shut up, you old soak!' Purdy suddenly roared. 'This ain't none of our business. I warned Dillon he was in for trouble if he went stirring up old man Hornstone. But he wouldn't listen. So you listen and listen good. No one helps Dillon. I don't want them Hornstone cowboys riding in here and going on a wrecking spree. We got a peaceable town here and I mean to keep it that way. So go on home and bury your head in a bottle.'

Solemnly the old man stared back at the person paid to keep the law in Gainsborough.

'There's a story in the Bible about a man beaten and robbed and left to die. A preacher came by and passed on the other side of the road. Then came a sheriff and he passed by also. A Samaritan saw the victim and came and ministered unto him. This town is an abomination on the face of the earth.'

'Get out of here!'

The door slammed behind the old man, leaving Sheriff Purdy muttering profanities after him. Back with the help-less victim Joe pulled ineffectually at the blood-soaked lariat. Dillon's blood had dried on the bindings and the old man could make no impression on the tightly drawn bonds. In desperation he walked the horse with its grisly burden down to the boarding house. He banged and rattled on the door but the landlady refused to answer his pleas. Wearying of his efforts Joe retraced his steps and his next stop was the livery.

'Charlie, you got to help me. I have a fella here what is likely to die if you don't give us a hand to get him off that horse and his hurts tended.'

'Hell, Joe, don't ask me to do this. I got a business to run. The bank owns the lease. I help that fella and I'm out on my ass.'

'So we just going to let him die cause we all afraid of the wrath of Hornstone?'

'Joe, I can't help you. Much as I would like to. But I just can't risk it.'

'Consarn it, but this is a goddamn rotten town. For two pins, if I had the stage fare I'd ride on out of this god-forsaken place.'

'Look Joe, you never heard this from me, but this morning Dillon went over to the store and loaded a pile of groceries into Amelia Huger's wagon. You know how she hates Hornstone. Maybe she might help.'

The liveryman went back inside and shut the door behind him. For a long time Joe stood looking at the closed door.

'Consarn it, if that's the way it has to be, so be it.'

Trying not to get too much blood on his clothes Joe grunted his way atop the horse.

'Now, old hoss, we got a mite of travelling to do.'

With Joe perched awkwardly on the horse in front of the bloodied Dillon, the trio clattered out of town.

10

Dillon awoke from a dark place and lay still, afraid to move in case the agony in his back worsened. He was lying on his face and it felt like his body was on fire. Along with the pain he could feel sweat leaking and running down his skin.

I am in hell, he thought. *All that killing I did while soldiering has landed me in this place.* He could not suppress a moan.

'I think he's awake,' a woman's voice said.

'With that back, maybe he'll wish he'd stayed under.' The second voice was a man's.

Slowly he opened his eyes and someone moved into his vision. Lying on his front he was at a disadvantage as he strained to look up.

'Mr Dillon, I need you to drink something. It won't be easy for you. Your back must be hurting bad. I got a jug here with a spout. Try and take in what you can.'

The jug was cold and tinny on his lips – deliciously cool. He sucked the jug dry.

'Thank you,' he croaked. 'How did I get here?'

'Joe brought you. You were hurting bad.'

'How long?'

'It's Thursday now, Joe brought you here Tuesday.'

'Thank you.'

'You must eat. I've made broth. I can use the jug again.'

Afterwards he slept.

The next day he forced himself to sit up and feed himself.

She had long tawny hair tumbling loosely to her shoulders. Her face was frank with a ready smile that had a dazzling effect when she turned it on him.

'Strange that we should meet again so soon. Thank you for taking me in and looking after me.'

'One good turn deserves another. What happened to you?'

'I went out to Hornstone and confronted them with my brother's murder. I'm certain Grant Hornstone killed him over a gambling debt. They beat me and tied me to my horse. After that I can't remember anything till I woke up here. I guess I owe you and Joe.'

'I was glad to help. Anyone who opposes Hornstone by that very fact becomes my friend.'

He was introduced to her son, a sturdy boy named Raoul. Joe had stayed on, not knowing what else to do. After what he had done he was apprehensive of going back to town.

'Joe, why'd you bring me here?'

Joe was twitching and Dillon guessed the old timer was going through the rigors of alcohol withdrawal.

'Consarn it, Captain, nobody would help. You came in town strapped to your horse, more dead than alive. I tried to get someone to help. They were all too frightened. Hornstone had warned them off.'

'I ain't a captain no more – just plain Tim.'

Joe was rubbing his arms and his head jerked from side to side.

'If I don't get a drink soon I guess I'll die. If I go back to town for a drink I don't know what they'll do to me for helping you. Probably sling me in jail. So whatever way the dice fall I'm in trouble.'

Dillon watched the woman move around. In spite of the pain in his back it was pleasing for him to watch. She had easy fluid movements and went about her tasks with quiet efficiency. When she caught him watching she blushed and smiled. He thought it was the most beautiful thing he had ever seen. Her hair was a wild tawny mess. She tried to comb some order into it with her fingers. It made no difference and he was enchanted. When she made the supper they all sat at the table together.

'Why are you helping me,' he asked.

'Because you needed help,' she answered simply.

Raoul watched him warily. Since his father's death no man had visited or spoken to them even when they went into town.

'We sure thought you were a goner,' the boy said. 'Who did it?'

'I met up with a bunch of cowboys. I told their boss his son had murdered my brother. So he had me flogged.'

'Was it Hornstone? He killed my pa.'

Dillon looked at Amelia. 'Like they killed my brother? Was it over cards?'

She shook her head. 'They lynched him for rustling.'

There was silence at the table while everyone concentrated on the food.

'He was framed. Hornstone's cowboys claimed they found him with a dead calf and took him into town to the sheriff. Next day they hanged him. There was no trial. It was a lynching.' She spoke simply and he could feel her pain.

'When I'm old enough I'm going to kill that cruel old man.'

Dillon looked at the boy, guessing he was about ten years old and here he was setting his life out on a course of vengeance.

'That day at the cemetery, I read what you wrote.'

'Every month we go in town and paint the crime on the

headboard. Every month when I return it's painted out again. I do it for Edward.'

'How do you manage here with no man to help?'

'My family send me a little money. It's sufficient to buy basics.' She gave one of her rare smiles. 'Occasionally a kindly stranger pays for groceries.'

'That was never enough for what you're doing for me.'

For a moment they were lost in each other's eyes. Then Amelia blushed deeply and looked down at her plate. Dillon looked across at Joe. The old-timer was pushing his food around the plate, probably wishing it was a bottle of bourbon instead of stew.

'Is Mrs Huger and Raoul in any danger for helping me?'

'We all are. Hornstone warned everyone to steer clear of you. That's why I had to come out here. You would have died otherwise. No one in town would help. They scared of what Hornstone will do to them.'

'What would he do?'

Joe shrugged. 'You work for someone you find yourself without a job. You got a place to live you get kicked out or maybe it burns down one night. If you owe money the bank forecloses your loan. Your friends stop talking to you or if they don't they get the treatment too. Hornstone riders hassle you. Traders won't sell to you. Most don't survive; they have to move on.'

'Guess I'd better move out. Don't want no one to get in trouble because of me.'

'You're going nowhere till you're fit.'

Amelia showed a touch of fire when she spoke then blushed and looked down at her plate again.

'How come they don't bother you?'

She did not answer, clearly uncomfortable with the question. Joe was shaking his head at Dillon, indicating for him to back off.

'Whatever, I'm grateful to you all. It seems to me I would be dead now but for the efforts of you and Raoul and Joe here.'

'Anyway, I got to be getting back to town,' Joe said. 'Things to attend to,' he added vaguely.

'You told me it wasn't safe.'

'Aw shucks, Hornstone can't do nothing to me. Sheriff Purdy might sling me in jail for a day or too. But I ain't got nothing anyway, so they'll more than likely leave me be. I'm just the town drunk. Hardly worth the effort.'

They tried to dissuade Joe from returning to Gainsborough, without avail. Dillon suspected that after these few days without a drink the old man was getting twitchy. The only transport they had was the mule-drawn wagon or Dillon's horse. So it was agreed that Raoul would ride Monday doubled up with Joe and drop him off near enough for the old man to walk into town; the youngster could then bring back the horse. Dillon gave the old man money. He knew it would be spent on booze but it would save him having to beg. Before he left Joe took Dillon to one side.

'You asked why Hornstone don't bother Mrs Huger,' the old man said. 'Story is Grant Hornstone was sweet on her. Pestered her to leave her husband and go to him.'

Tim stared at the old man, shaking his head. 'What you trying to tell me?'

'You figure it out yourself. Don't take no brains.'

11

Joe's first port of call was the Bottom Dollar where he ordered a bottle of bourbon. The barkeep glared malevolently at him.

'Get out of here, you mangy old swill belly. I told you afore not to come in here smelling up the place and annoying customers.'

'Man, if you ain't the orneriest goddamn piece of horse dung. All I want is a bottle. I ain't drinking it in here in this flea-joint. I'm taking it back to my place where I don't have to look at your ugly mug. Enough to make a fella swear off likker.'

'Shut your goddamn mouth and get the hell out of here afore I take this blackjack to you.'

A bunch of cowboys were watching the argument with some amusement.

'What's all the fuss, Harry?'

'Oh, howdy, Mr Hornstone. Ain't nothing I can't take care of. I'll serve you soon as I got rid of this old reprobate.'

He leaned over the bar and whispered something in the ear of Grant Hornstone. Hornstone nodded thoughtfully. He reached out and patted Joe on the shoulder.

'Howdy, old-timer. I hear tell you helped a fella as was badly beat up. That was mighty noble of you. Can I buy you a drink?'

Joe flinched under the touch of the young man's hand. 'Eh, what?'

'I bet you drink bourbon. Harry, set up a bottle for our friend Joe here. Ain't every day you meet a good kindly fella like Joe.'

Smirking, the barkeep did as he was told. The cowboys gathered round grinning as they anticipated some fun. One of crowd reached to help himself. Hornstone slapped his hand away.

'Leave it. That's Joe's bottle. Harry, another couple of bottles and glasses. Joe and me and the boys are going on a drinking spree tonight.'

It was a jolly party at the bar as the whiskey bottles rapidly emptied. Joe drinking greedily in case his good luck ran out. He was wary at first of Hornstone but as the drink took hold he mellowed. Maybe this Grant Hornstone weren't as bad as people said.

'Where'd you take him, Joe?' The question came unexpectedly.

'Huh.'

'I said: where did you take that Dillon fella?'

'Who said I did any such thing?'

'Everybody says. The whole town knows. So I'll ask you once again, where did you take Dillon?'

'Dunno, cut him loose – put him on his hoss and sent him on his way. Could be anywhere by now.'

Hornstone nodded to his men. Two of them took an arm apiece and spread-eagled Joe against the bar. The first punch hit the old man in the gut. His mouth opened wide, he wheezed and gasped trying to suck in air. Before he could recover the second and third blow landed. He hung moaning and dribbling snot, held upright by the men on either side. Grant reached over to the bar, picked up a bottle and drained it.

'Set 'em up again, Harry.'

'Sure thing, Mr Grant.'

There was silence in the saloon as people watched an old man being beaten by a bunch of cowboys. No one protested. No one came to his aid. Joe's battered old hat had fallen to the floor. Grant pushed Joe's head upright.

'Tell me Joe. Where is Dillon? Then you can go on with your drinking.'

'I don't know nothing, Mr Hornstone,' Joe wheezed. 'I'm just an old drunk as minds his own business.'

'Harry, can I borrow your nightstick?'

'Sure thing, Mr Grant.'

Gleefully, Harry handed over the thick black cudgel he used to keep order amongst unruly customers.

'Where did he go, old man?'

Grant stepped back a pace, raised the truncheon and brought it down hard on Joe's outstretched arm. The old man screamed as his arm was broken. The club rose and fell again and then again. Grant started on the knees next. A man can only stand so much punishment. In the end Joe told Grant Hornstone what he wanted to know.

'Throw him outside.'

Ignoring his screams they grabbed the old man by his bust arms and tossed him in the street. He lay in the dirt moaning, unable to stand because of his smashed knees. One of the cowboys thoughtfully tossed Joe's hat into the dirt beside him. With both arms broken the old man could not raise himself up. Moaning pitifully it took him an age to roll under the boardwalk, where he passed out.

Inside the Bottom Dollar Grant Hornstone sat thinking about the information he had beaten out of the old man. After ordering another bottle he stumped upstairs to one of the bedrooms and fell asleep in the arms of a saloon girl.

Night closed down over Gainsborough. An old man lay dying in the street but no one went to look.

When Raoul got back home Dillon busied himself checking over Monday and his rig. Amelia came out to watch.

'You going somewhere?'

He turned and nodded. 'After what Joe told me what happens to folk as help Hornstone enemies I have to move out. I don't want to bring trouble on you.'

'Trouble? What more can they do to me?'

'You got Raoul to think about. I don't want it on my conscience either of you were harmed on account of helping me.'

'Where will you go?'

'Those hills are within easy riding distance. I can camp out there.'

Dillon put his foot in the stirrup and swung up on the saddle. She saw his face crease with pain.

'You're not properly healed. You're welcome to stay a few more days.'

'Mr Dillon,' Raoul piped up. 'You going to get Hornstone for killing your brother?'

Dillon shook his head. 'I reckon not, Raoul. Hornstone has too many riders working for him for me to get anywhere near him. I'll hide out in the hills till I'm healed, then head on out.' He didn't look at Amelia as he spoke.

'You're a liar, Tim Dillon. You're not a man as quits and runs. You're not leaving, are you?'

From the top of his horse he gazed down at her. Raoul came to stand by his mother and together they stared up at him.

'Wait.' She went in the house and after some time re-emerged carrying a couple of rolled-up blankets along with a packet of food. 'You'll need something to keep you warm.' From her skirt pocket she pulled a Colt .38. 'Take this; I notice you ain't got any arms.'

He hesitated before taking the gun and tucking it in his waistband.

'Thanks. My weapons are back in Gainsborough. I stored my kit at the livery. Probably all my stuff is looted by now. I should have asked Joe to look out for them.'

She watched him ride away and had a bad feeling inside, like the time she'd had to ride into Gainsborough to see her husband in jail. She had been too late. The horror of that day still caused her nightmares. They had left him hanging and no one came to help. She had to cut Edward down and then bring him to the undertaker all on her own.

Dillon did not go far. He camped a few miles away, wanting to be on hand if anything happened. No matter Grant Hornstone having a yearning for Amelia; from all he had seen the Hornstones were an outfit of ruthless hoodlums, doling out punishment with impunity to anyone who crossed them.

Dexter had money he'd won from Grant Hornstone and he was killed for it. Edward Huger had an attractive wife whom Grant coveted, and he was killed also.

Seems to me in this country you want something you take it at the point of a gun. There's fellas robbing trains and banks and being hunted down for it. Here they kill and steal and no one takes any heed.

12

Grant Hornstone woke in the bedroom of the Bottom Dollar saloon, groaned, rolled over and stared at the woman snoring beside him. Make-up had smeared or been rubbed off, exposing the ravaged face of the saloon gal. A feeling of disgust welled up in Grant, followed by a surge of rage.

'Get the hell out of here,' he bawled.

He punched and shoved the woman who, startled out of her sleep, began to swear back at her attacker. A fist hit her in the mouth and she fell backwards out of the bed, landing on the floor.

'Get your goddamn ass out of here!' Grant yelled at her.

The rage on her face changed to one of fear when she awoke to where she was and who it was she was with.

'I'm so sorry, Mr Hornstone,' she mumbled before grabbing up a wrap and scuttling for the door.

'And get some coffee sent up,' Grant shouted.

As he thrashed about in the bed his hand encountered a bottle. When he held it up to the light he could see it was empty. With a snarl he hurled it at the terrified woman, who was fumbling with the door. The bottle bounced off her head, eliciting a startled scream, then fell to the carpet. By then the woman had the door open and sobbing loudly she scuttled outside. Hornstone lay back in the bed, his thoughts turning to Amelia Huger.

'Stupid bitch, she could have had me and now all she

has is a miserable hutch as ain't worth riding out to,' he muttered. 'Now she gone and taken that drifter in. Well, we'll see about that.'

There was a discreet knock on the door and a head poked inside.

'I got coffee and bourbon here, boss.'

'Jason, come on in. I got a head as feels like a woodpecker is inside trying to hammer its way back out again.'

The cowboy pushed inside balancing a tray that held a whiskey bottle and a coffee pot.

'Could do with some of this myself. I must have drunk a gallon of bourbon last night. Then the damn whore kept me up half the night talking. Danged if she would shut up.'

As Jason talked he filled a mug with half coffee, half whiskey, handed it to Hornstone, then served himself with the same mix.

'Hell, Jason you don't know how to handle females. They're like horses. You got to break them in. Show them who is the boss. A heavy hand with the whip soon teaches them who's in charge.'

'I ain't much good at neither, boss. I always managed to find me a broke horse to ride and I reckon the same with females.'

'Soon as we breakfast we're heading out after that Dillon fella. This time we do the job proper.'

'Hell boss, he shouldn't have survived only that old coot rescued him. What a goddamn old fool to go interfering in stuff as is none of his business. I reckon he's regretting it now. But why you bothered about some saddle bum?'

The old coot Jason was referring to was long past regretting anything. He was stretched underneath the boardwalk where he had crawled last night and had died of his injuries during the hours of darkness.

'Can't you see? He's shacked up with the Huger woman? I ain't having her getting cosy with some drifter. If I can't have her no one else can. She had her chance to come to my bed and spurned me. No one does that to Grant Hornstone. I'll make her live to regret her decision to reject me.'

'Hell boss, she's a sparky filly. Last time we went near the place she started firing off that rifle. She's going to hit some of us one day if we keep on going out there.'

'Yeah, well this time we take Purdy with us. He can arrest her for harbouring a fugitive. A few days in the cooler will take the starch out of her.'

'Damn good idea. She ain't likely to start shooting with the sheriff there.'

A couple of hours later Grant Hornstone and a half-dozen cowboys, accompanied by a reluctant Sheriff Purdy, were riding out to hunt for Dillon. Jason's estimate of Amelia Huger's willingness to cut loose with her rifle proved prophetic. Having always to be on the alert for incursions from Hornstone she never strayed far from her firearms. Though she had given Tim a revolver she still had her rifle and, when she caught sight of the approaching riders she went inside the house, grabbed up her rifle and from the protection of the doorway loosed a few shots over their heads.

'That's far enough. State your business and then get the hell off my land.'

'Sheriff,' Hornstone snarled, 'tell her.'

'Missis Huger, Sheriff Bill Purdy here. We're hunting a wanted man. We have reason to believe he is holed up here.'

'No one here, Purdy, just me and my boy. So if that's all you're after no need for you to linger.'

'Jason,' Hornstone hissed, 'Take a couple of men and

circle round. See if you can sneak up back.'

Jason obediently reversed his horse and he and two other cowboys backed away down the trail and out of sight.

'What you up to?' Amelia called. 'Where those fellas going?'

'Tell her we're sending for reinforcements and to let us search the place.'

'I'm sending back to town for more men. You save yourself a lot of grief if you just let us come on in and search.'

'Keep her talking.'

'Ma'am, if you got nothing to hide I suggest you just do as I ask. It'll only take a short time for us to look. Right now you are committing a felony by obstructing the law.'

'Law! What law? My husband was murdered and you showed no inclination to do anything about it. I suspect you helped hang him. There was no trial, no chance to defend himself. That's the sort of justice you serve out. Now you come out here bothering his widow.'

'Ma'am, I ain't figuring on bothering you none. I'm just trying to do my job.'

'Huh, that'll be a first. What's this fella done you're after, anyway?'

The sheriff turned to Hornstone with a frown. 'What'll I say?'

'Tell her he's wanted for murder. You got an arrest warrant from – hell knows where.'

'He's wanted for murder. I got a warrant come in from Kansas City so I have to serve it.'

There was a sudden yell from inside the cabin, a shot, and then struggling figures appeared in the doorway.

'Yippee, he got her.' Hornstone yelled and urged his horse towards the house.

His two remaining men followed with an unhappy lawman trailing behind.

The cowboys were trying to subdue a flushed and angry Amelia. Jason held her round the waist from behind while another cowboy was tugging at her gun. By the time the riders reached the yard it was all over. Another cowboy emerged from the cabin dragging Raoul with him.

'What are you doing? Leave my boy alone.' Amelia yelled. 'This is my land. You're trespassing.' Then she turned her spleen on Hornstone. 'I might have known. You're behind all the evil in this county. Murderer!'

Sheriff Purdy came up slowly. 'Ma'am, I have to ask you in the name of the law if you have knowledge of the where-abouts of the wanted criminal, name of Dillon?'

'I see no law here – only back-shooters and women beaters and murderers. And let my boy go.'

Hornstone slid from his horse and began to roll a smoke, taking his time. The riders dismounted and gath-ered in the yard, no one speaking, waiting for Hornstone, watching him work the tobacco and paper. It was only when he finished and was lighting his cigarette with a lucifer that he opened his mouth to speak. At that moment a there was a movement from the side of the yard. Hornstone with remarkable dexterity whipped out his gun and fired several shots. There was the crash of a heavy body falling. Amelia twisted round to see what had happened and her eyes went wide with shock.

'Pickaxe! You shot my mule. Oh God, no!'

'Pickaxe!' Raoul called, his face a tragic mask of horror.

The cowboys were standing round grinning.

'Nice pistol work, Mr Hornstone.'

'Sure taught him a lesson.'

'Sure as shooting that mule won't go sneaking up on no-one no more.'

'All right, all right.' Hornstone was grinning along with the rest of his hands. 'Search the place. See if there's anyone else skulking about.'

'There's no one here but me and my boy.'

'Is that so? We heard different. Heard as that outlaw what you were so friendly with at Blakemore's store was hiding out here.'

Understanding came to her as he spoke.

'Joe,' she whispered. 'Oh God, not that poor old man.'

Hornstone was smirking as he pulled on his smoke.

'Had to hurt him a mite, but he told us in the end.'

The cowboys were coming back in the yard. Some had searched the house and others the outhouses. One carried a torn and bloodied buckskin shirt.

'Found this in the washhouse, but no other sign.'

Hornstone eyed the ruined shirt. 'Guess I better have a look myself.' He disappeared inside the house.

Amelia struggled against the strong embrace of Jason. 'Let me go, you bastard.'

'Tut-tut, such language from a lady. Whoever would have believed it?'

She tried to slam her head back into her captor's face but he only laughed as he easily avoided the blow.

'I like it when they struggle. Gets me all roused.'

There was the crash of breaking glass from inside the house that got everyone's attention. Amelia stared apprehensively over her shoulder and a few moments later Hornstone reappeared. He was grinning widely.

'My cigarette went out and when I tried to relight it I knocked over a lamp.' Smoke drifted out behind him. 'Goddamn thing started a blaze. I couldn't find anything to put it out.'

'Damn you!'

Amelia increased her struggles, staring in horror as the smoke curled into the doorway.

''Better get everyone to safety. Don't want no one to get

burned now.'

They dragged the protesting woman and her son back up towards the gate. A tongue of yellow flame could be seen licking at the curtains. More and more smoke poured from the doorway. There was a sudden detonation as a window exploded.

'Yippee! That sure is a burner.'

Tendrils of smoke were crawling from the roof and it wasn't long before flames could be seen flickering among the shingles. The house was mostly built of timber. It was not long before the whole structure was a raging inferno.

13

Dillon couldn't get the image of Amelia Huger out of his head. Hazel eyes gazed earnestly out at him and more than once he had to rein in his imagination.

That young woman sure got under my skin. Damned shame what happened to her husband. He must have been one fine hombre to win such a wonderful woman.

Then he would get angry thinking what Hornstone had done to her family. But anger wasn't Dillon's way. Cool, calculating and steady he had always been and that had stood him in good stead in the army. In hostile situations he was the one with the calm head figuring out the odds. Sending out scouts to probe the strength of the enemy, whether it be Indians or Mexican raiders or outlaw gangs before making any rash moves.

Quite often against his superior's orders he would take

on the scouting missions personally. He learned a lot from these encounters and endured hardships and privation to penetrate enemy positions and bring back information on deployment and valuable estimates of the dangers of each assault. His raids against the enemies of the United States of America were virtually always successful, with minimum loss of life to his own troops.

The more astute commanders would bow to his judgement, knowing that the success of their command often rested with such men. And he never let them down. Captain Tim Dillon was a born fighter and tactician. When he eventually led his men into a battle it was a fight he was reasonably confident he could win.

Now that he understood how Hornstone operated he knew his best plan would be to ride far away from here – and the further the better. He had fought against men equally vicious, callous and ruthless in the past and he knew there were no limits to their barbarity.

But in those fights he had had a unit of the United States Cavalry to back him up. Here in this remote part of Oregon he was alone, with every man's hand against him except for a few brave people like Joe and Amelia. If it became known that they had aided him then Hornstone would come down hard on them. From what he had learned of Hornstone the more he realized the man would make an implacable and merciless enemy. To survive in this corner of the world you unequivocally accepted Stirling Hornstone as your lord and master and his word as law. As Dillon ruminated on the events of the last few days he noticed the smoke; a great billow of grey-blue rising into the sky. For a moment he stood contemplating it.

Damnit, I'm sure that's in the direction of the Huger place.

Quickly Dillon saddled up, slung himself on top of

Monday and headed in the direction of the smoke. Nearing the farm he could see that his fears were correct, for the smoke was indeed coming from the location of the Huger place. As he neared he could hear the jangle of horses; immediately he slowed Monday to a walk and paced cautiously towards the farm. As he came in sight of the yard he pulled up.

What the hell. . . .

The farmhouse was well ablaze, flames shooting out of the roof and jetting from windows and doors. Then he saw the two figures standing in the yard. Amelia had her arm around her son and they were staring at the conflagration consuming their home. Slowly he walked his mount towards them. Raoul noticed him first and pointed. Amelia watched him ride on in.

'I take it this was no accident?'

She shook her head, her face pale and stricken. 'Hornstone and his crew.'

'They were looking for you,' Raoul piped up. 'Ma said she didn't know where you were.'

'I'm sorry; looks like I bought a load of trouble on you.'

She shook her head. 'It was bound to happen sooner or later. I was a thorn in their side. While I was still here I reminded everyone what Hornstone had done to Edward. It didn't help none that I rode into town every month and wrote up the crime on his gravestone.'

There was a crash from the house as the roof timbers collapsed, sending up flaming debris and swirling smoke. They all stepped back as the heat from the burning house intensified. When Amelia looked back at Dillon he could see despair in her face.

'They held us while they searched the house and then Hornstone set it ablaze. Sheriff Purdy stood by and let it all happen. I realize now the danger I was putting Raoul in.

I've lost my husband. I don't want to lose my son. They could easily have shot us both and put our bodies in the house so there would be no evidence of the crime. No one comes by here so we would probably have lain here for months before being missed, if ever.'

'Ma, don't worry about me. When I'm bigger I'll go after Hornstone. I'll get me a gun and shoot him like he shot Pickaxe.'

Amelia ruffled his long black hair. 'I know you would, son. But then they would hunt you down and do the same to you.'

Suddenly he pulled away from her, his face tight and angry. 'You can go, but I ain't going nowhere. I'll stay and fight.'

'Raoul, you saw what they did today. We were helpless. They'd think nothing of gunning down a young boy and even less his mother. You're only ten. You've got all your life ahead of you.' She turned to Dillon who had remained silent during this exchange. 'Tell him, Mr Dillon.'

'Your ma's right, Raoul. We would need an army to take on Hornstone. He must have at least a hundred riders working for him. You saw what he did to me when I went to confront him. Someone who has that much power would hardly bat an eyelid when using it. They just snap their fingers and their gunhands do the dirty work.'

The boy looked dolefully at the two adults, then turned and began kicking at the dirt, his shoulders slumped in an attitude of dejection. Dillon looked across at Amelia.

'Raoul said they shot Pickaxe. Who was Pickaxe?'

'Our mule. It just shows how mean and vicious they are. Pickaxe was our only means of transport.'

Amelia splayed her hands then let them fall to her sides, her face desolate. She was like a lost child seeking comfort. Dillon had to restrain himself from reaching out and taking her in his arms.

'I got to go in town and pick up my belongings. I left some at the livery stable and some at the boarding house. Then I'll come by here and help you do whatever you got to do. Maybe I can pick up another mule for you.'

Her eyes widened. 'You can't go in there. Hornstone tortured Joe to tell where you were. I forgot to tell you.'

'That old man was just a harmless drunk.' Dillon turned and stared in the direction of Gainsborough. 'First they murder your husband, then murder my brother and now they beat up on Joe and burn down your house. The debts are mounting and will have to be settled.'

The last sentence was uttered so low that Amelia couldn't quite make it out but she didn't ask. In spite of her entreaties Dillon was determined to go into Gainsborough and collect his possessions; that was if they hadn't already been stolen.

14

In case someone was on the lookout for him, Dillon circled round the town so he came in the opposite direction, and cantered up to the livery. Charlie came out to attend the rider and stopped short. He began to back away.

'Howdy, old-timer. I come to pick up some property I stored with you.'

'You get them quick and then sashay out of here pronto, mister. I can't afford no trouble having dealings with you.'

Dillon winced as he dismounted. All this riding had aggravated his damaged back. He was far from recovered from his flogging.

'I just want what's rightfully mine. No more, no less.'

Charlie kept glancing nervously up and down the street. Dillon ignored him and went inside the building. His bedroll was as he had left it and he undid the leather straps that held it together. A Remington rifle and a gun rig with a Navy Colt in the holster lay exposed. The liveryman was getting even more agitated as he watched Dillon buckle the gunbelt and adjust it. With a slick movement the Colt was in his hand. Charlie stepped back a pace and watched wide-eyed as Dillon checked the loads, then replaced the weapon. The Remington was given the same treatment. The gun given to him by Amelia he left tucked in his waistband.

'What do I owe you for storage?'

'Nothing, mister, nothing. Just go.'

Dillon frowned at the man. 'You were a friend of Joe's?'

'No, I got no friends. Please mister, I'll lose everything if I'm seen helping you.'

'Tell me what happened to Joe – then I'll leave.'

'Jeeze, I'm a dead man. They beat Joe to death. Broke his arms and broke his legs and threw him out in the street. He lay there in the dirt moaning – everyone, including me, afraid to go to his help – then he crawled under the boardwalk and died.'

For long moments Dillon gazed at the liveryman. 'You wouldn't treat a dog any worse,' he said at last.

'You're right, mister. You don't think I feel ashamed of myself?' Charlie shrugged helplessly. 'We're like a town of insects. We crawl around scared of our own shadows; terrified we might do something to annoy the Hornstones.

And they laugh and ride roughshod over us and we cringe and take it.' He was shaking his head and tears rolled down his cheeks. 'Joe didn't deserve that. Joe was a good man. He might have been the town drunk but he was a better man than anyone in this goddamn rotten burg.'

Dillon walked outside, loaded his bedroll on Monday, then took up the reins thinking it would be easier walking than trying to climb aboard again with his stiff back. His next stop wasn't far, anyway. He led Monday around the side of the store and ground-hitched him. Blakemore looked up, his smile of welcome fading. His face paled also.

'Sorry, we're closing. No more trade today.'

Dillon put a written list on the counter. 'Mister, I'm in a hurry. I know you don't like me but the sooner you fill that list the sooner I'll be gone.'

'You don't know what you're asking. I serve you then I'm a dead man.'

'You're the second man to tell me that. This town must have a lot of dead men walking around.'

Dillon picked up a gunnysack and began filling it with his order while Blakemore watched him, nervously licking his lips.

'Cartridges? I don't see any. I need ammo.'

'Out back, I keep it separate.' A look of cunning appeared in the storekeeper's face. 'I'll fetch it.' He said it too eagerly and turned to leave.

'That's all right, I'll come with you. I have a good idea of what I want.'

In a short while Dillon filled two bulging gunnysacks.

'Tell you what, Blakemore; I'll do you a favour. I ain't going to pay for these supplies.' The storekeeper was too scared to reply as Dillon continued: 'That way you can claim I robbed you. When I'm gone you can report the robbery to the sheriff and Hornstone can't blame you. What can a man do if a fella sticks a gun in his ribs and demands the goods? Would it help if I were to hit you over the head? Make it look like you put up a fight.'

His face as pale as the chalk he sold, Blakemore sank into a chair and put his head in his hands.

'Just go. I think I'm going to pass out.'

Dillon hefted his supplies, walked over to the door, stepped outside on to the boardwalk and stopped. There were five of them standing in the road: Hornstone cowboys, thumbs hooked in gunbelts grinning maliciously at the man emerging from the store.

'Well, lookee here, if it ain't that fella as we whupped last week. Looks like he's hankering after another dose of rawhide.'

'Some fellas are like that, can't get enough of a good thing.'

'Are we going to do it here in town or should we take him back to the ranch and let Grant have the pleasure?'

Dillon, his hands weighed down by the overflowing gunnysacks remained silent, weighing up the opposition.

'We'd better take him back. Boss mightn't like us hogging all the fun to ourselves.' The speaker, a big cowboy with a full ginger beard, appeared to be the leader. 'Mister, you going to come quiet or do we have to pistol-whip you and tie you on your horse?'

'Don't suppose you fellas would reconsider and just let me go on my way, peaceable like?'

Ginger was shaking his head, grinning gleefully. He pulled his pistol, casually aiming at the man on the steps of the store.

'No way, mister. Grant wants your hide and what Grant wants Grant gets. Now, like I say you can ride with us astride your horse or tied face down and a few dents in

71

your skull. Don't mind which. Your call.'

'I guess you have me cold.' Dillon raised the gunny-sacks. 'I guess I won't be needing these.'

He tossed the bags out into the road and the cowboys, taking their eyes off the man on the boardwalk, looked at the goods spilling into the dirt. Cans of beans, sacks of flour, muslin-wrapped fatback.

As the produce tipped out Dillon snatched the revolver from his waistband and shot Ginger. The big man staggered back, blood blossoming on his shirt front, his mouth and eyes wide open in shock. But Dillon had already lined up a second cowboy and fired again at the man in the plaid shirt. Two down, and the other three shocked and frightened cowboys were bringing up their guns.

The big man on the store veranda was merciless. He emptied his gun and it dropped from his hand. Before it bounced on the boardwalk he snatched his Navy Colt smoothly from the holster and continued firing.

The silence was almost palpable after the shocking noise of firing. Gun smoke drifted from the front of the store where Dillon was standing, shooter in hand, watching the street for reinforcements coming to back up the cowboys. Nothing stirred and a kind of hush hung over the town.

The silence was broken as one of the wounded cowboys cried out. Another one was moaning. Still carrying his gun Dillon turned back into the store. A shocked Blakemore was still sitting where Dillon had left him, his eyes wide and terrified in his pasty face.

'Mr Blakemore, I sure would be obliged if you would go out in the street there and pick up my things. I had an argument with some cowboys and in the course of the dispute the sacks got spilled.'

Dillon stared coldly at the storekeeper. Shaking visibly, his eyes never leaving the gun in Dillon's hand, Blakemore managed to get to his feet and stumble outside. Trying not to look at the tumbled heap of bodies in the street, he began to gather the goods and refill the gunnysacks.

'Help me,' a cowboy cried out. 'For gawd's sake someone help me.'

Amidst the carnage a man was sobbing helplessly.

Remaining inside the store, Dillon reloaded his Navy Colt and pouched it. He stepped outside and retrieved the revolver from the boardwalk. Keeping a wary eye on the street Dillon reloaded this weapon also. There was still no sign of activity in the town.

The storekeeper finished his task and stayed where he was, balancing the now refilled gunnysacks beside him, afraid to look at the terrible nemesis that had come into his town and caused such devastation. Dillon whistled. Monday perked up its head and obediently trotted round the corner.

'Tie them on my horse,' Tim ordered.

Ignoring the blood-soaked heap of bodies and without another glance at the storekeeper Dillon walked his horse back down to the livery. Charlie peered fearfully out at his visitor.

'You got five Hornstone ponies stabled here.'

'Yes, sir.'

'They won't be needing them no more. I want them saddled and ready to go.'

The citizens of Gainsborough watched fearfully from behind closed doors as the tall stranger led a string of horses from the town.

15

The parlour of the Hornstone ranch house was lavishly furnished with padded chairs and sofas and glass-fronted cabinets against the walls. A huge open fireplace took centre place with logs stacked either side. Stirling Hornstone stood before the fire, stiff as a ramrod, his face suffused with rage. Grant stood before his father, hunched over and staring at anything rather than meet his father's glare.

'What the hell is going on? How come this saddle tramp can ride into my town, rob my store and gun down five of my hands? And then ride out again taking five of my cow-ponies with him?'

'Joe Briggs took him out to the Huger place. We went out there for him but he had bolted.'

'You useless piece of garbage. How the hell did I father such a brainless, spineless weakling? Sometimes I wonder if your ma didn't stray a mite when you were born. That would explain a lot.'

There was more withering scorn poured out on his son. Grant stood, white-faced, staring at the carpet. There was another person in the room but he took no part in the exchange between father and son. Sheriff Purdy stood near the door as if considering the best moment for his escape.

'Hell, Pa. As I recall it was you as ordered him whipped and tied to his horse and sent on his way. Me, I would have finished him off good and proper. I would have strung him up on the nearest tree. We wouldn't have this bother now.'

'This Dillon fella rode into my yard with some cock-and-bull story about his brother. Said he won money from you in a card game and you killed him to get it back. Even you wouldn't be that stupid.'

'Hell no, Pa, there weren't no card game. Ask any of the boys that were with me that night.'

Stirling's eyes narrowed. 'What night?'

'Why, the night of the card game,' Grant blustered, realizing he had blundered but not quite knowing how. 'The boys an' me, we just drank a few beers and played billiards. Some of the fellas wanted to take the whores upstairs but I weren't having none of that. I wanted to get a good night's sleep so as I would be up early to go over to Preston and buy them cattle you were after.'

'Something tells me you're lying, but then you always were a lying son of a bitch. Now get yourself out in that yard and rustle up a bunch of those no-account hands. Make sure they're armed, and pick fellas that ain't afraid to shoot a lone gunman.'

Grant turned to the door but before he opened it his father had one more instruction for him. 'And Grant, I know you're sweet on the Huger woman. Seems to me she's the cause of a lot of this bother. I'm sick of her making all those allegations against the Hornstone outfit. Sheriff Purdy will arrest her for making false accusations against us. Either that or you silence her permanently.'

'Sure, Pa. I'll take care of it.'

Sheriff Purdy made as if to follow Grant but Stirling stopped him with a wave of his hand.

'Shut the door, Purdy, I want a word with you. Tell me what the hell is going on. And I want the truth. I get the idea you been covering for Grant but just remember who it is that pays your wages.'

'I ain't sure of all the facts, Mr Hornstone, but as far as I know it's just as Grant says—'

'Purdy!' The name whipped out like a gunshot, making the lawman jerk. 'So help me, if I don't start hearing some truth from you then you better start looking for another job.'

The sheriff had been standing with his hat in his hands and began nervously kneading the fabric.

'I . . . I don't want to say anything as seems to contradict Grant, but I'll tell you as I see it.'

Hornstone said nothing, glowering at the man before him, making Purdy even more nervous.

'There was some talk about a card game one night and this young fella, Dillon, won a sizeable amount of money. Grant accused Dillon of cheating and called him out for a showdown in the street. Dillon made a run for it and next morning he was found dead.'

Hornstone was staring at a point somewhere above Purdy's head when the sheriff paused. 'Then Dillon's brother showed up and started asking awkward questions, making out Grant had something to do with the killing of his brother. I warned him off but he weren't satisfied. He rode out here and from what I heard he was flogged and tied to his horse. The horse turned up in town. No one was going to help but the town drunk hauled him out to the Huger woman. From what I know she took him in and tended his wounds.

'When Grant heard this he went crazy and beat the old man so bad he died. Next day we all rode out to the Huger place and Grant set fire to the house. Then this Dillon *hombre* rode into town, made Brownlow load him up with supplies. Some of your boys were still in town and they faced down Dillon as he came out of the store.' Again the sheriff paused in his narrative to glance nervously at his boss.

'Go on.'

'Dillon, he took them on, all five, and gunned them down in the street. Three dead and two badly wounded. Went down the livery, made Charlie saddle up their ponies and rode out.'

'Where the hell were you when all this was going on?'

'I heard the shooting, but by the time I armed myself and got down there it was all over.'

The sheriff shifted nervously on his feet, his fingers working at his hat.

'By the time you armed yourself and got down there it was all over,' Hornstone sneered. 'My guess is you hid till it was safe to come out of your gopher hole.'

Purdy stared at the carpet, unable to meet the rancher's contemptuous gaze.

'What a goddamn mess! In future when Grant messes up you come straight to me. No more covering up or lies, or by God you'll end up behind your own bars. You get this sorted. I don't care how. I want this Dillon rannie dead and buried, I don't care how. And I want that Huger woman out of my hair one way or the other. If it means another killing then so be it.' For long moments Hornstone gazed hard at his pet lawman. 'Now get the hell out of my sight.'

Sheriff Purdy found Grant Hornstone assembling a party of cowboys. He cast his eye over the posse.

'How many?' he growled.

'There's forty good men, all armed and ready to go hunting.'

'They know who they're after?'

'Sure thing, I've told them it's the fella as gunned down

Ginger Jackson and his boys. They're pretty riled up about it.'

Sheriff Purdy rose in his stirrups. 'Men, this *hombre* we're hunting is one mean son of a bitch. As you know he's already killed some of your pals. He's a mad dog on the loose. We need to take him down. When we catch up with him, shoot to kill. There may be a female with him. Don't let that bother you none. If she gets hurt in the crossfire – too bad. A female like that ain't of no account. She has no regard for her good name or her safety so she deserves whatever comes to her. Everybody clear on what we have to do?'

His answer was a savage howl as a score of cowboys bawled out their righteous anger.

16

Amelia heard the horses and immediately took cover behind the wagon, calling Raoul to join her. She grabbed up her carbine and slid a bullet into the breech.

'Get in behind me,' she ordered Raoul.

The boy's face was as determined as was hers as they waited, fearing the worst. They knew it could not be Tim arriving. More than one mount meant only one thing. Hornstone had returned with his cowboys.

'What devilry do they plan now?' she muttered, squinting along the barrel of the rifle. 'This time I'm shooting first and asking questions after.'

They had been busy in the interval, salvaging what they

could from the ruins. It was very little for so much effort. Fortunately the outhouses had escaped the fire and they packed tools and farming implements – in fact anything that had the remotest use. Most of their household possessions had been burned to blackened ruin so anything that could be salvaged was a welcome addition to the miserable collection of usable items. Amelia frowned, hardly believing her ears. Someone was singing.

'It was down in ol' Kentucky, I met young Maggie Duffy.
She had a belly on her like a poisoned pup.
I drank her home-made likker from out a porcelain cup,
And by gob she looked so pretty through the empty demijohn,
And by gob she looked so pretty through the empty demijohn,
I asked that gal to marry me . . .'

The singer hove into sight and broke off his singing when he caught sight of Amelia and Raoul.

'Howdy, ma'am, I was feared you would put a bullet in me if I arrived unannounced. Never heard of no one shooting a singer. Though once down in Kansas was a fella whose singing was so bad the audience shot at his feet and he danced so well he discovered a whole new talent. Runs a troupe of dancing gals now and is doing right well for himself.'

By now Dillon was in the yard with his string of cow ponies. Getting over her surprise Amelia came from behind the wagon with Raoul and stood looking at him in bemusement.

'What on earth have you been up to?'

'Well, as he burned down your house and shot your mule, I figured Hornstone owed you a mite, so I took these here ponies to kind of make up for your loss. Not the same, of course, but they'll do as a down payment.'

Amelia was staring in bewilderment at the little drove standing contentedly in her yard, all saddled and bridled, complete with saddle-bags and rifles pushed into scabbards. She gazed shrewdly back at him.

'Surely he wouldn't have given them up willingly?'

'No, but don't you bother your head about such details,' Dillon replied. He patted the gunnysacks slung on the ponies. 'We even got ourselves a whole new load of supplies, compliments of Mr Blakemore. I see you were loading the wagon; were you thinking of going somewhere?'

Amelia glanced across at her son, who was excitedly examining the cowponies.

'Hornstone has won. I'm leaving. For myself I don't care what they do. But I fear for Raoul; I'm taking him away from danger.' She gestured around at the still smouldering house. 'There's nothing left. It was hard enough before, now it will be nigh on impossible to make a living from this place. We were living from hand to mouth as it was. You saw how the storekeeper treated me. Everyone around here is the same. There's no future in this blighted place for Raoul. It isn't fair that I keep him here, hoping to bring justice for my murdered husband.'

'Mr Dillon,' Raoul called. 'Is it all right if I sit on one of these ponies?'

'Raoul, you pick the one you like best and you can have him.'

Raoul's rounded eyes said it all. 'This one.'

'Try him for size.'

In a moment the boy was aboard the pony, grinning across at the adults.

'Take him up the trail a piece, but don't go far.'

Dillon turned back to Amelia and saw the tender look in her eyes as she watched her son ride out of the yard. There was soot on her face and she was sweaty and dishevelled and Dillon's heart turned over in his chest. He had to stop himself from reaching out and touching her.

'You're right to move out,' he said. 'My guess is Hornstone will come out here again looking for me. I figure this time he won't stop at shooting mules and setting fire to things.'

'What are you saying?'

'Ma'am, I've come across some mean critters in my time but the Hornstones are a whole new breed unto themselves. They gave poor old Joe a savage beating, then threw him out in the street to crawl away and die like a dog. No one went to help for they were all afraid of what Hornstone would do to them.'

His eyes were bleak as he spoke her and she sensed a hardness in the man, which gave her an inkling of how he had acquired a string of Hornstone ponies.

'I struck a blow against them today. Their pride and poisonous nature means they can't let that go. It would be a sign of weakness on their part. This time when they come for me they'll come shooting. So, even though it is me they're hunting, if they find you and Raoul here they'll more than likely hurt you. It's in their nature to bully and beat up on folk weaker than themselves. So I figure we should head out into the hills and find a place to hole up where evil-tempered ranchers won't bother us. That'll give us a breather while we think of some way of getting you and Raoul to a place of safety beyond the reach of Hornstone.'

For a moment he was lost in a pair of hazel eyes that were slightly tearful.

'You're a good man, Tim Dillon. I take it you'll be

leaving with us?'

He turned away. 'Maybe.'

'Ride 'em cowboy!'

Raoul's shrill yells saved him from elaborating further as the youngster, his face flushed with excitement, came trotting back into the yard.

'You know this area better than me. Is there somewhere we should head for that'll keep us hid from Hornstone's people?'

Amelia pursed her lips and frowned into the distance. 'There's an old abandoned mine. Ed and I went exploring up there once. It was all neglected and looked like no one had been out there since the mine closed. It's remote and there are derelict shacks and outbuildings we may be able to fix up to give us shelter.'

Within half an hour from Dillon's return the convoy set out. One of the new ponies had been harnessed to the wagon to replace the dead mule. The surplus ponies were tethered to the rear of the wagon. Raoul, proudly riding his new mount, rode alongside the wagon with Amelia in the driving seat.

'You lead the way, ma'am,' Dillon instructed. 'I'll watch our back trail.'

Dillon had cut a large bush and used one of the lariats he had obtained along with the ponies to trail this behind him in an attempt to obliterate traces of their tracks. He was hoping Hornstone didn't have an expert tracker amongst his cowboys.

When the riders came storming on to the little ranch all they found were the smoking ruins of the family home and the carcass of an old mule. There was no sign of the people they were hunting.

'Search all around,' yelled Grant. 'They must be

here somewhere.'

The cowboys spread out, combing the surrounding area. There were enough of them to conduct a thorough search. After all, they were used to scouring all sorts of terrain for stray cattle. They were experts at this kind of thing. An hour later Sheriff Purdy suggested they call the search off.

'It's getting dark. I suggest we call time on it and start again in the morning. My guess they've gone into the hills. Could be anywhere.'

They gathered by the ruined ranch. Grant glared at the place, wishing there was something he could vent his anger on. But there was nothing. The place was a ruin and the people he might have been able to brutalize were gone. Angry and frustrated he gathered his men and rode away. In the gloom they did not notice a lone rider following. If they did they probably imagined it was one of their own trailing behind on a lamed horse.

17

Dillon kept several hundred yards behind the bunched mass of Hornstone riders. He felt safe for he was beginning to understand the make-up of his enemy. Arrogant and bullying, they felt very secure in the power of the fear and intimidation they aroused. Theirs was an unassailable position. Who would dare challenge the power of Hornstone? They had cowed the populace over which they held sway. Dillon's understanding of this was why he had been able to take on five Hornstone gunnies and take them down.

They had not been expecting resistance. They were Hornstone cowboys; five of them against one man. Their people had already beaten and flogged this saddle bum. He should have taken the hint and crawled away and died. But he hadn't, so when they found him in town they expected Dillon to roll over and allow them to take him back to the ranch and a certain and painful death.

Confident and cocksure, they had been off-guard. The distraction with the spilled gunnysacks was just an extra ruse to give Dillon that added edge. No one bucked Hornstone so the cowboys had been unprepared for Dillon's savage and unexpected attack.

Dusk settled indolently across the grasslands and details became blurred. Dillon closed up the gap between him and the bunched cowboys. When he judged he was a couple of hundred yards behind the riders he pulled up Monday and slipped his Remington rifle from the scabbard. He dropped to the ground and steadied the weapon on the saddle.

His target was the dark mass of riders riding unsuspectingly towards their home ranch and a comfortable bunk. They would be out in the morning again to continue the hunt for the lone man who dared to stand up against the might of Hornstone.

This was no occasion for accurate shooting. Dillon commenced firing, sweeping his rifle in an arc that ranged across the throng of mounted cowboys. Monday, a well-trained cavalry mount, stood rock steady as the rifle boomed out. The horse might have been carved from wood for all the movement it made as the gunfire erupted.

There were no individual targets to be picked out. Dillon was shooting into a mass of riders and hoped he might score with almost with every bullet. He emptied the magazine, leisurely reloaded, pouched the rifle and swung back on board. He wheeled his horse and cantered into the obscurity of the night away from the chaos he had created.

Behind him he could hear loud shouts and cussing mingled with screams and the terrified neighing of spooked or injured horses. Shots were fired, but Dillon knew the frightened cowboys were firing blindly into the night. Steadily he rode till he neared the hills where he had left the Huger family making camp at the abandoned mine site.

When he spotted the campfire he called out his name before riding in. As he dismounted he could smell coffee.

'Coffee smells good.'

'Is that a hint you got a thirst?'

'I guess you got me figured out, ma'am.'

'Mr Dillon, would it be too much for you to address me as Amelia? I don't know how long we'll be here but it seems we could be on first name terms at least.'

'Sorry, ma'am, I mean Amelia. And I would be obliged if you call me Tim.'

'Now that's settled. Tim, are you hungry?'

He smelt the fatback and his tummy rumbled loudly.

'Begging your pardon.'

She giggled. 'I see you're a man as don't mind expressing his feelings.'

He squatted down by the fire, glad she could not see his blushes and surprised she could still find laughter after all that had happened.

'I see you made yourself at home.' He glanced round and spotted the shape of the sleeping boy. Tethered near by was a pony. He grinned into the gloom. 'That boy will make a good trail hand. I see he sleeps with his mount handy.'

'I had to practically drag him off the thing. Insisted on having it close while he slept. Mind you, I think the feeling is mutual. The animal seemed reluctant to part from Raoul. They've become big pals. Thank you for giving it to him. A boy's first pony is a big step up in the world.'

Tim looked across at her, glad she couldn't see his discomfiture in the gloom.

'I . . . you know how I came by them?'

'I could smell gun smoke off you when you returned. It seems stronger tonight. Where have you been?'

She handed him a plate and a fork and he began to eat. It was a while before he answered:

'When I rode into Gainsborough today to collect my stuff, I intended to do just that. I went in to the store and loaded up with the things I thought you might need.'

'You were mighty thorough: pots and pans and all a gal needs to live in the wilderness.'

'It was a good job you moved out. Hornstone came back again. He must have been pretty riled when he found you were gone. They hunted about for a while but the sun was beginning to set so they rode away. I expect they'll start searching again in the morning.'

'Tell me about Gainsborough.'

'When I stepped out of the store they were waiting for me. They gave me a choice. I could come willingly or they would drag me back to Hornstone on the end of a rope. Either way I knew I was a dead man. I shot them down like the dogs they were. As they wouldn't need their ponies again, I thought it only fair to impound them.'

'You brought five ponies back – does that mean there were five of them?'

'I reckon.'

'You shoot them all?'

'I figured they might be the ones as beat Joe and threw him out into the street. No one dared come to his aid. He lay in the dirt and died with no one to help him. For years Hornstone cowboys have been riding roughshod over the citizens of this god-forsaken place. They didn't expect a lone man to fight them. I had the advantage of surprise. They're bullies and so cocksure they didn't expect no one would oppose them.'

'Tim, that's not why I asked. I wasn't questioning your actions. I just wanted you to tell me, is all. You think I don't know what kind of men the Hornstone cowboys are? You called them bullies and cowards. And you are right. What other kind of men would come out to a lone woman and burn her house down around her ears?' Then she added as an afterthought: 'And shoot her mule.'

He chewed on his food and the silence grew between them. Firelight flickered on the two figures both sunk in their thoughts.

'What about tonight? You say they came back.'

'I followed in the dark and shot them up a mite.'

He could almost feel the intensity of her stare across the fire. He finished his meal, set the plate down and reached for the makings.

'You mind if I smoke?'

'I used to roll them for my father. Would you let me see if I have lost my skill?'

Dillon looked up in surprise, but tossed her the tobacco sack and she began to build him a smoke.

'Ma would tell him off but he took no mind. He would never let me puff on it even though I wanted to.'

Her head was bent over the task and Dillon wanted this

moment to last; the firelight playing on her hair, the woman patiently rolling a smoke for him. It was a pleasurable feeling of contentedness. Something that he had not experienced in a long time – not since his boyhood, and then maybe not even as good as at this moment.

'In all these years you are the first man to stand up to Hornstone. He'll come for you. And being the coward he is he will come with his pack of bullyboys at his heels. What are our chances?'

She handed him his smoke and he lit it from a burning ember. Pulling contentedly on the tobacco he did not want to think of revenge-seeking ranchers, but he spoke because she had asked.

'Yes, they'll come all right. Tonight I attacked out of the dusk. Hopefully I killed or injured a few of them. They'll be jumpy and scared and a mite wary. That should slow them down some. Tomorrow, first light, we'll hide everything inside the mine. Remove all sign of our being here. One of us will be on watch while the other two work. If Hornstone gets this far they mustn't suspect we're here. But we must prepare for if they do discover us. It's a good spot, for there are high places to keep a watch from and also to fire down on an enemy. We have plenty of weapons and ammo. We're going to stash them up in the rocks so at any time one of us can scramble up there and put down fire on the attackers. I'm hoping it won't come to that. But it's best to be prepared.'

'I never asked, but what did you do before you came out to this hellhole?'

Dillon blew smoke out into the night air. 'I was a captain in the United States Cavalry. Dexter sent me to come and open a saloon with him. I had money saved and he reckoned he had a bankroll to finance the deal. I was going to be a high-rolling saloon owner.' His brief chuckle was wistful. 'Probably Dexter had me marked out as his barkeep.' She could hear his sigh. 'I guess I'll never know.'

18

The little camp was up and bustling with activity almost before the sun rimmed the surrounding rocks. After breakfast Dillon directed their preparations.

'We hide all our gear out of sight. Put the wagon inside the mineshaft and anything we may want to use in one of those old ramshackle sheds. From now on we can't light any fires. We'll just have to eat cold.

'Raoul, ride down the valley a piece and see if you can find a place to hide the horses – somewhere sheltered and grass to keep them content. Hornstone's cowboys may come up here and they may not. If they just give the place a casual once over it has to look deserted. But if they do discover us we must make it so hot for them that they'll retreat. We've plenty of weapons and ammunition that came with them cowponies Hornstone so kindly donated. And I brought back more boxes of bullets from Blakemore's store.'

He pointed up on the rock rim above the mine. 'I'm going to climb up there and place rifles and ammo, so if we have to retreat we can shoot down on them. It'll give us some advantage.' He paused. 'Hell, if you can think of any-thing I missed just yell out.'

'You seem to have everything in hand, Captain.'

He smiled back at Amelia, impressed by the way she was standing up to the hardships imposed on them.

'Just plain Tim will do, Amelia. I'm a civilian now.'

'Seems to me you're still thinking like a soldier.' She waved her hand around. 'All these preparations. Have you taken into consideration that Hornstone outnumbers us about a hundred to one?'

Dillon nodded soberly. 'That's the only advantage he has. But bear in mind that in just one day Hornstone suffered losses of several horses and men. I've no way of knowing how many casualties I inflicted in last night's attack – maybe another five. So that's ten men down. The cowboys coming out today will be worried they're going to be next in the firing line. If I know waged men, they won't be too eager to fight if they know they're going to get hurt.'

By mid-morning Dillon was convinced they could do no more to make the camp secure.

'We'll take turns keeping a lookout. There's a ledge by the entrance to this gorge. From there you'll be able to see anyone approaching. Divide up the watch between yourself and Raoul for now. I'm going to take a ride out and see what's happening.'

'Be careful, Tim. You're our only hope. If it wasn't for you, either Raoul or me or both of us might be dead.'

'Huh, if I hadn't come here and interfered none of this would have happened.'

'Hush, I wouldn't have it any other way. At least we can give Hornstone a bloody nose.'

'Oh, I intend to do more than that. I'm determined to hack away at him till I bring down the Hornstone organization. After all, it is built on fear. Once people see he's just an ordinary man and can be hurt the tide will turn.'

She watched him ride away with some misgivings.

On two occasions Dillon had to hide from groups of riders who, he guessed, were members of the posse searching for him. They had obviously split up into smaller groups to widen the range of the search area. He had learned a few tricks at concealment from his time of hunting Indians. At a single command Monday would subside to the ground and lie flat in the grass till ordered back on his feet again. Tim would do likewise, making both horse and rider invisible to the casual observer.

He rode many miles that day, scouting the land and learning where the searchers were concentrating their efforts. He hoped to find a smaller group of cowboys that he might attack, but each time he spotted riders they were in numbers too great for one man to tackle.

It was a frustrating day, with nothing much accomplished, but he came across vast herds of cattle, often unattended or with just one or two cowpokes. He kept his distance from them, and if on occasion he attracted attention from the cowboys he would wave a greeting, but ride on casually till he was out of sight.

Seeing cattle in such numbers sparked off an idea of striking a blow against Hornstone. He mulled over the plan as he ranged wide across the grasslands, figuring out the lie of the land. Satisfied he could make his plan work he headed back.

At the entrance to the area of the old mine he paused and cast an eye over the place. He was pleased to see that while he had been away Amelia and Raoul had been busy tidying up; and he could detect no obvious sign of human occupation. As he rode up towards the mine entrance Raoul rose up behind a bush that was growing halfway up the rock face. He waved to him. Amelia appeared from behind a derelict shack and awaited his arrival.

'You're probably hungry. I can only offer you cold

beans and fresh bread.'

'Fresh bread – how'd you manage that?'

She pointed to the mine entrance. 'I went in there and found a place where I could light a fire. I didn't think it would do no harm seeing as the smoke drifted down into the back of the mine.'

'You're full of surprises.' He was smiling as he spoke.

'I made a pot of coffee also. Wrapped it in burlap sacks to keep it warm. It won't be piping hot but it's better than a cold drink.'

Inside the mine entrance he sat on an upturned crate and ate beans and bread washed down with a couple of mugs of warm coffee. As he dined he told her about the riders hunting them.

'My guess is they pulled in cowboys to join the hunt. Instead of riding herd they are out hunting us. Which gives me the glimmerings of a plan whereby I might be able to strike a blow against Hornstone. While his cowboys are out hunting me the cattle are being neglected. I might be able to work that to our advantage.'

'What have you in mind?'

'I have an idea to use Hornstone cattle as a weapon. I got to work out the details yet but I believe I have a reasonable chance of success.'

'What will be the end of this?'

Dillon didn't answer straight away. 'When I've destroyed Hornstone,' he said eventually.

Amelia was watching him as he spoke, saw the bleak look in his eyes, and shivered.

'I'm a reasonable man. I went out to his ranch, unarmed and wanting to sort this thing out. He swatted me like I was a horsefly as was bothering him. My brother was a piece of dirt to be swept into the gutter. They tied me on my horse and sent me out to die. That way they could plead ignorance of my fate. Had it not been for Joe and you their plan would have succeeded. They wanted information from Joe so they beat him to death. They found out you had helped me so they burned your house down. The way I see it Hornstone declared war on me and my friends. I understand war. I spent a goodly number of years learning all about war. I was good at it. This war is a war to the finish. Only one of us will be still standing when it is over.'

'But you are only one man.' Amelia broke the silence that had sprung up after Dillon's declaration of war on Hornstone.

'Let me tell you the story of a man called Gerontur.'

19

'Gerontur was chief of a small Indian tribe. One day a gang of miners raided his village and slaughtered everyone living there. They wanted the land, you see. Someone had found gold near by, so they massacred the people who might object. Gerontur was away from home that day. When he returned and found what had happened he gathered together the survivors of the massacre and took them to a place of safety. Then he declared war on those miners.

'Gerontur was one man. Some nights he crept into the miners' camp and killed men as they slept. At other times he shot fire arrows and burned their property. He set mantraps for the men foraging for wood or out hunting. He dug pits in the road so supply wagons bogged down, and he shot the drivers as they worked to get going again. The miners set night guards and Gerontur crept up on them and slit their throats. They organized manhunts but Gerontur melted away and they found nothing. While they were out hunting him Gerontur raided their camp and slaughtered the few men he found there.

'That mining camp is derelict now. The miners fled the nemesis they had called down upon their heads. I can live out here and make raids on Hornstone. I'll make him rue the day he tangled with the Dillon family. I shall have my revenge.'

He suddenly stopped talking and attempted a smile, but the hardness remained in his eyes. 'I'd better relieve Raoul before he becomes too disgruntled. I don't think I am capable of dealing with a cantankerous youngster who thinks we've forgotten him.'

Amelia watched him climb up the narrow rocky path and saw Raoul stand up to greet him. Dillon settled down behind the bush and Raoul remained talking to him. A great sadness overwhelmed her as she watched the man and her son together.

'You need a father, Raoul,' she said wistfully, 'but maybe not a man who is skilled in war.'

She thought of her dead husband and wondered whether, if he had been more warlike, he would have survived. But she knew otherwise. Like Dillon said, Hornstone treated people like insects to be swatted if they got in the way. Only a man like Tim Dillon was capable of dealing with the Hornstones. He had been a soldier and had a life of fighting behind him.

Tears welled as she was overwhelmed by sorrow. She was under no illusions. Edward had died because Grant

Hornstone had wanted her. They would get Dillon also. It was only a matter of time. Hornstone had the overwhelming numbers. Dillon was just one man. Well, maybe one man, a woman and a boy. But what good was she and Raoul in a campaign of this kind? She watched her son climbing down from the rock face.

'Ma, Mr Dillon said I was to go and look to the horses. He wants me to take Monday and put him with the others.'

'That's fine. You needn't hurry back. You'll want to spend some time with your new pony. Have you given him a name yet?'

'I sure have, Ma. I called him Pickaxe II.'

She laughed. 'Seems fitting, though he seems a mite faster than the original Pickaxe.'

'Them Hornstones, they kill everything, don't they, Ma. They killed Pa, they killed Mr Dillon's brother and they killed Pickaxe.'

'Yes, I'm afraid so. They're a pretty mean bunch, all right.'

Suddenly he wrapped his arms around her. 'I'm glad Mr Dillon is here. He's going to look after us.'

She stroked his head as she held him. She hoped Raoul was right. He released her and, taking Monday's reins, led him away. Dillon had insisted that they should keep the horses separate from their own living quarters.

'That way if we are attacked we can retreat to the horses and make a run for it.'

Amelia turned and wandered back into the mine. The shaft ran more or less straight into the core of the hill. She lit a lantern and explored further back than she had ventured so far. She came across occasional rusted tools but nothing of interest till she saw the boxes stacked against one wall. She set the lantern on the floor and brushed at the dust with her fingers in an effort to read the faint writing on the lid.

DYNAMITE Handle with care No naked lights.

Moving very slowly Amelia picked up the lamp and reversed away from her discovery. She had no idea if there was anything inside but she was too scared to pry further. It was only when she was outside in the fresh air again that she felt safe.

'And to think I was lighting fires in there,' she muttered. 'I'd better warn Tim and Raoul about it.'

That evening, after a cold meal washed down with water Dillon opted to take the first watch.

'I'll wake you an hour or two after midnight,' he told Amelia. 'If you do a few hours, then wake me and I'll take over till dawn.'

Dillon was gritty-eyed as he watched the colourful pink and red hues of dawn edge over the rim of the gorge. He yawned widely, remembering similar vigils in the past when he had watched for marauders.

Nothing changed, he thought. Here I am on guard duty again but this time without a company of cavalry to back me up.

He had let the woman and the boy sleep on. Amelia had looked so exhausted before turning in that he had not the heart to disturb her.

'Hell, she had her home burned down and then had to flee into the hills and set up camp again in this miserable place. A good night's sleep will do her the power of good.'

He was full of admiration at how she had stood up to the hardships that had suddenly beset her, all because she had helped him when he was in sore need. She had surely saved his life.

When the sleepers finally woke up Amelia berated Dillon for not waking her.

'We were supposed to share the watch. It would have

been no hardship for me to stand guard for a few hours.'

'I guess I must have fallen asleep,' Dillon lied.

'Which just goes to prove we all have to do our share.' She took in his red-rimmed eyes and tired look. 'You ain't fully recovered from that whipping. You're doing far too much. You need to rest up.'

Dillon yawned widely, then excused himself. 'I reckon I better get some shuteye during this lull in the hunting season. Before that I'd better have a look at that box you found marked dynamite. If there's any left it might come in handy if we have to fend off an attack.'

20

'I'm going out to scout around. I want to know how many men Hornstone has out hunting us and where he is concentrating the search. A good general has to know the enemy's movements and where his troops are congregating. I have a few ideas as to how to sting Hornstone. I aim to whittle away at him till his men become edgy and maybe some might pull up stakes and move on. After all, cowboys are just hired hands. If things get too dangerous or look like getting out of control the uncertainty will unsettle them. Most of them were hired to punch cattle, not to fight a war.'

Before he left the foothills and ventured into the grasslands Dillon took a glass from his saddlebag and scanned the horizon. It was a while before he caught sight of the faint dust cloud far out on his right. He studied this for some time and when he discerned the direction in which it was headed he plotted his own course. Before he left the camp he asked Amelia to draw him a map of the area, putting in the Hornstone ranch and Gainsborough and indicating their own position. He was looking for something in particular and had asked Amelia the most likely place he would find it.

'Cattle, there are vast numbers of Hornstone cattle ranging all over. You won't ride far before you run into them.'

Having set Monday to a ground-eating canter, Dillon continued out on to the flats. As he rode Dillon took note of the lush grass over which he travelled. Cattle would fatten and thrive well on these rich grasslands. He had not told Amelia why he wanted to know where to find cattle but he had a special purpose in mind for them.

Soon he could see the evidence of livestock having passed. Cow chips and flattened and chewed down grass indicated the signs of a sizeable herd. When he saw movement up ahead he angled towards the mass of cattle coming into view.

He presumed Hornstone would have herds like this scattered all over his range and, while it would be difficult to keep track of all of the beasts, he supposed the rancher's reputation for rough justice would have kept rustling low. He could see riders with the herd and continued to watch them, but as far as they were concerned he was just another cowboy and he didn't attract too much attention.

Keeping an eye on the sky to give him his bearings Dillon began angling Monday in the direction he wanted. When he thought he was in the correct position he reined in the horse, consulted a compass, then rode another couple of hundred yards to the right.

'Mmm, that looks about right, Monday. Now we're going to see what kind of cowpony you make.'

The horse shook its head and whickered, almost as if in understanding. Dillon chuckled.

'Just don't you be going and putting your hoof in no gopher hole, you hear? Or we're both dead meat.'

Though there was not a cloud in the sky Dillon took out his rain slicker. Urging Monday in amongst the grazing cattle he shook the slicker, the stiff material making a cracking, snapping noise. At the same time he uttered a weird ululating sound he had learned from a Navaho brave. The Indians used it when stalking an enemy and a warrior told Dillon it terrified their opponents so much that when they heard it they usually ran away. Now Dillon had the opportunity to find out if it worked on cattle.

The wildly flapping cape and the weird sounds Dillon produced were making the cattle nervous. Those nearest scattered out of the way of this strange creature and his bizarre behaviour. Dillon continued shaking away at his slicker and more and more of the beasts were becoming restless. Some were starting to trot away from him. Cattle were bumping into those in front and this in turn was agitating more and more of the beasts. Some began bellowing and the calls were taken up by other cattle further away.

Dillon worked hard, shaking the slicker, feeling the soreness in his back as he did so, which only served to remind him of the fate that awaited him should he be caught by any of the Hornstone men.

The couple of cowboys riding herd had realized that something was wrong and were moving into the herd in an attempt to calm the cattle. One of the riders was waving and shouting something and pointing towards Dillon, but by now the noise from the cattle was so loud no words could be heard. The cowboy began angling his pony towards the newcomer.

There would come a point at which the panic induced in the beasts would reach a critical stage and they would begin to run. Seeing the cowboy urging his pony through the cattle with the obvious intention of accosting him Dillon decided to accelerate the process.

He pulled out his Colt and fired into the air. It was the last straw that speeded up the herd's nervousness. The sudden loud explosions were all that was needed to push the cattle over the edge and they stampeded. Dillon could see the herders' futile attempts to stop the onrushing steers, but it was too little too late. There was no stopping that headlong dash.

Whooping and yelling Dillon kept up the pressure at the rear of the herd. He was beginning to enjoy himself.

'Goddamn, Monday,' he yelled, 'you're a natural. We been wasting our time all those years in the cavalry. We could have been out here in Oregon chasing cattle.'

And indeed the big cavalry horse entered into the thrill of the chase and raced madly along, keeping pace with the herd. In the dust and confusion kicked up by the stampeding cattle Dillon lost sight of the cowboys. He swung wide of the herd determined to keep it running in the direction he wanted. But in the end there was nothing he could do to influence it. The mass of beasts had a mind of its own; nothing short of exhaustion or some natural barrier was going to stop them.

He fired off another chamber of bullets for good measure, then eased up Monday and watched the herd thunder on. He had loaded the cannon and fired it. He could only hope that the shot would hit its intended target.

21

Stirling Hornstone stepped on his veranda. He pulled out a cigar and lit it from a Lucifer struck against an upright and stared out through the clouds of smoke.

'Useless, cowardly snivelling son of a bitch,' he raged, giving vent to a string of colourful epithets that called into question his son's mental ability and manliness. 'I keep losing men as well as the time they spend hunting that saddle tramp. This is a working ranch and needs someone to spend time looking after livestock and a hundred and one things now being neglected. While all that useless son of mine has done is chase a will o' the wisp.'

Grant had cringed before the old man, his own rage and frustrations overwhelmed by the sheer venom pouring from his father. Not for the first time Grant considered killing his father. Sometimes he imagined standing in front of Stirling and putting bullet after bullet into that contemptuous face. Sometimes he could almost see the blood and see the old man tumbling to the floor, his hands pressed uselessly over the wounds.

Why, Grant, why, why'd you do it?

And in his daydream Grant would emulate the contemptuous sneer that was the usual expression on his father's face when addressing his son.

I did it because you're an old done man – not fit to hold down this ranch no more. It's time a younger man took over. Old men are past history. Oh, and try and not get too much blood on the carpet. But maybe I'll probably change it anyway. I'll be changing a lot of things around here and not before time.

Stirling Hornstone was not given to daydreaming as was his son. The cattle baron dwelt in the real world where he had accumulated wealth and territory by sheer ruthlessness. There wasn't an ounce of softness in the man. He had done his share of killing and thieving to get to where he was. Anything that remotely threatened that position was mercilessly suppressed and if that meant riding roughshod over competitors Stirling Hornstone had no hesitation in doing so. His thorniest problem, though, he had not been able to deal with.

'How the hell did I breed a halfwit son?' he growled into the cigar. 'There's none of me in the brat.'

Not for the first time he wondered if his wife, dead these long years, had somehow strayed and Grant was the son of some inferior strain.

'Times I'm tempted to put a bullet in his brain and put us both out of our misery. Then again, maybe he ain't got a brain and the bullet would go straight through and let some sense in his skull.'

Chivvied by his father, Grant had organized the cowboys into groups and sent them out to begin another hunt for the man who was bringing mayhem to Hornstone territory.

'You scour the range and find him. You either kill the son of a bitch or bring him back here to be hanged, but either way I want this sorted.'

'Sure Pa, I know what I'm doing. We'll get him all right. I promised the men a bonus at the end of this.'

'What the hell you do that for? There's plenty of work to be done around here other than chasing after troublemakers. They get paid to do a job. No goddamn need to give them extra.'

Now the ranch boss fumed impatiently on his veranda, smoking his cigar and staring into the distance.

'A bonus!' he snorted once or twice.

As he turned to go back inside some disturbance in the distance caught his attention. It was almost imperceptible but a man who grew up in the outdoors, herding cattle, developed a sense for anything out of the ordinary that might disrupt the general course of his calling. Hornstone stared hard into the distance, sensing an interruption in the placid nature of the day. There was turbulence in the air that did not seem quite natural.

'What the goddamn hell. . . !'

A glance at the sky showed no signs other than those of a normally calm day. No hint of thunder or storm clouds. It was the wrong season for tornadoes. His ears picked it up then – a faint rumble in the distance. The rancher frowned. He thought he could feel a trembling or a vibration beneath his feet. He stepped off the porch on to the gravel path and stood staring at his boots. He could feel it now – a definite tremor beneath his feet.

'Earthquake?' he mused.

The rumbling was getting louder and he stepped back on the veranda the better to look towards the sound. He noticed that some of the hands had stopped their work and, like him, were staring out towards the source of the disturbance. A couple of them had clambered on the top rails of the corral and were peering into the distance, their hands shading their eyes.

As Hornstone squinted out over the grasslands he thought he could discern a dark wave low on the horizon and above it dust swirling into the air in a murky cloud. He began to get an ominous perception of what was happening

'Henry,' he called over his shoulder to his servant,

'bring my glass.'

The rancher extended the 'scope and focused on the phenomenon. It took him a few moments to realize what he was seeing.

'Goddamn, it's cattle on the rampage,' he roared, collapsing the glass and tossing it to his servant. 'Warn everybody. Tell them to saddle up and get out there.'

Then he realized how short of men he was. The bulk of his cowboys had been drafted in for the manhunt. Henry took off running towards the bunkhouse; his boss quickly following him.

'Goddamn stampede. It had to happen now when everyone's away.' Panting heavily he arrived at the corral. 'Get saddled up. Stampede heading this way. We got to try and stop them or turn them away from the ranch.'

The crew assembled at the gate – pathetically few. The menacing thunder of hundreds of hoofs pounding the dirt had become much louder and the oncoming herd was now in plain sight. The dark surging tide was approaching the ranch at a frightening rate.

'Come on,' Hornstone yelled, 'spread out. We won't be able to stop them but maybe we can turn them.'

He urged his horse out towards the surging tide of beef, his men following reluctantly. The rancher took off his hat and began to wave it as he charged towards the oncoming herd.

'Get back, you sons of bitches!' he yelled.

He might as well have whistled a lullaby for all the notice the maddened cattle took of the man who owned them. On they came. Then, from somewhere in the distance behind the stampeding cattle, he heard the sound of gunshots. Suddenly it dawned on him that this was no accidental happening. Someone was driving the herd – deliberately stampeding them – and he had a good idea who it was.

A rider was catching up with him, racing beside him, yelling at him, but the noise of hundreds of panicked longhorns drowned out the words. The cowboy reached out and grabbed Hornstone's reins, pulling his mount around in a circle.

'What the hell. . . ?!'

Then they were running for their lives as the mass of livestock flowed relentlessly forward. Back through the gateway under the big iron sign announcing to the world that this was Hornstone; the cowboy did not let go of the rancher's reins till he had rounded the corner of the ranch house and pulled in behind it.

The longhorns smashed into the barbed wire, the front row of the beasts going down, entangled in the fence; their companions trampled over their carcasses, pounding them into the dust. Some fortunate few had followed the cowboys in through the gate, but others smashed into the uprights. The proud iron sign tottered and leaned, then gave way, crashing to the ground. More beasts went down and were mangled in the pile-up.

They smashed everything in their path. Corral fences disintegrated and terrified ponies were either trampled or some lucky ones fled before the heaving mass of steers. The herd poured over the ranch, flattening everything in its path. The tide parted and flowed around the ranch and outhouses, then carried on running. The beeves had much more running to do before exhaustion set in and they stumbled to an exhausted halt many miles from their starting place.

22

Tired and dispirited, the search parties were returning to Hornstone to find a scene of desolation. The once orderly and busy ranch was a ruin. The corrals and holding-pens were smashed out of existence beneath the hundreds of hoofs that had swept through the property, leaving only matchwood in their wake. Dotted here and there amongst the wreckage were the carcasses of cows and horses, some trampled out of recognition. On the veranda of the big house were stretched two tarpaulin-covered shapes.

Stirling Hornstone was directing salvage operations with the few hands who had been retained at the ranch while the bulk of the cowhands were out on the manhunt. He watched bleakly as his son approached.

'I take it you ain't caught that son of a bitch?'

Grant was shaking his head, staring round at the devastation. When the searchers left this morning this had been a fully operational ranch, with corrals and holding-pens filled with livestock and men working at the numerous tasks necessary to keep the huge cattle business functioning.

'While you were out chasing that son of a bitch he stampeded the herd right through my ranch.'

'Jeeze, I'm sorry, Pa. I can't believe this. It's . . . it's like a scene from hell. Dead animals and everything kicked to mush.' Grant pointed to the tarpaulin-covered shapes stretched out on the veranda. 'Am I right in thinking you got a couple of dead men?'

'Josh Casey and Larry Porringer.' The rancher turned bleak eyes on his son. 'I've had enough of this pussyfooting around. I've given you enough time to bring that son of a bitch in. I'll find someone as will do the job for me.'

'Hell, Pa, it's like looking for a needle in a haystack. He could be anywhere out there.'

Hornstone didn't deign to reply but turned away and addressed the cowboys who had come in with Grant.

'You men, I want this place back to working order. Half of you start clearing up this mess, the rest go out there and round up those longhorns as stampeded through here.'

Men, weary after spending a fruitless day in the saddle and looking forward to a meal and a rest, were suddenly drafted in to carry on working. Disgruntled as they were, no one dared express his dissatisfaction aloud. All were aware of the foul temper of the rancher and knew he was capable of venting his anger in a physical manner.

They had seen recalcitrant hands subjected to fists and boots and on more than one occasion the lash, and no one wanted to draw attention to himself by grumbling, so they divided into teams and began the thankless task of cleaning up.

Amelia and Raoul watched Dillon ride in and pull up before the mine entrance before showing themselves. Horse and rider were so covered in dust as to be almost unrecognizable. Dillon climbed down from Monday and grinned across at them, his teeth showing up starkly white against his dust-coated face.

'What on earth have you been doing?'

'Chasing cows,' Dillon replied enigmatically. He slapped Monday on the rump, raising a dust cloud. 'I think we both could do with a bath.'

He took off his hat and began beating at his clothing,

producing more dust to drift into the air.

'I've seen birds having dust baths,' Amelia called, 'but it's the first time I saw a rider do the same. It's a good job we are living in the open air. I would never have let you into my house in that condition.'

'I might die of thirst amongst all this dust. I guess I could drink a well dry.' Dillon picked up a canteen and took a long pull. 'My, but that tastes mighty fine. Given the choice I'd as sooner have a beer from the Bottom Dollar. But there's as much chance of that as there is of that churlish barkeep giving me my room back.' He turned and gazed at the horse. 'I suspect Monday feels the same.' At that point Dillon couldn't prevent a huge yawn.

'Oh, Tim, you're done in. Let Raoul take Monday and attend to him while you get some rest.'

'Sure thing,' Raoul piped up. 'I can wash him as well if you like.'

'Heck, it's a lot to ask.'

'I don't mind.'

Again Dillon yawned. 'Sorry about this. I come all over weary of a sudden.'

'You're doing too much without proper rest and you haven't recovered from that beating.'

'Well, maybe you're right. I guess I could do with a mite of shuteye.'

'That's settled then. You have a sleep while Raoul takes care of Monday.'

Raoul walked over and took the reins from Dillon. Amelia could see the man was almost out on his feet. He smiled at Raoul, then trudged towards the mine where the bedrolls were stored.

'No need to tell you to be on the lookout for Hornstone riders,' Amelia admonished Raoul.

'I'll be careful.'

Amelia watched her son walk along the track towards the enclosure they had made for the horses. She climbed the path to the lookout platform. With Tim inside the mine and Raoul busy with the horses she thought she'd better do her stint of guard duty to make up for missing out on last night.

When he finished sluicing down Monday Raoul decided to take him for a ride. Feeling very important the youngster sat atop the big horse. Monday was a well-trained mount and sensing the inexperience of the young rider the horse cantered along, responding to the lightest touch of reins or heels. Curious about the state of his old home Raoul set course towards his former abode.

23

Sheriff Purdy scratched under his arm and yawned. He could hear his stomach rumbling and his eyes felt gritty from lack of sleep. The burden of the night's guard duty had fallen on the sheriff, for as soon as the search party had arrived at the Huger place Hornstone had spread his blankets and lain down amongst the trees. The three cowboys who had accompanied them promptly did the same, leaving the lawman to stay awake and keep a lonely watch.

Purdy had been afraid to awaken Hornstone or his cowboys. After all, this venture had been his idea and it was up to him to make sure someone kept watch. Lacking the authority to order Hornstone's cowboys, the sheriff had no option but to stay on guard all night himself.

In the aftermath of the stampede and the chaos that ensued Sheriff Purdy had taken Grant to one side and had voiced his thoughts regarding the hunt for the renegade Dillon.

'I figure it all centres on the Huger place,' he confided. 'If you can spare me a couple of men I'll go back there and stake out the place. There's a chance the woman or Dillon might call there again. They left in a hurry and might come back to collect something or other.'

'Hell, I'm tempted to go with you myself. With the old man in such a foul mood I'd as soon not be around at the moment. He's bad enough when things are going smoothly, but right now he's like a bull with a hot iron up its ass.'

The two men corralled another three cowboys, then the group sneaked away without attracting the attention of the ranch boss. At the burned-out Huger ranch, after establishing that no one was there, they set up camp where they could keep an eye on the yard.

'We take turns keeping watch. If nothing happens in the night one of us will ride into town and bring back breakfast.'

As morning crept on Grant Hornstone awoke in a bad temper, cursing the sheriff for taking them on this hare-brained scheme. He ordered one of his men to go into town and bring back food and drink. Hornstone had relieved himself amongst the trees, lain down again and gone back to sleep, leaving the sheriff to continue his lonely vigil.

'What the hell am I doing, at my time of life sitting in an alfalfa patch watching out for someone hard to pin down as a damned raccoon? You look for him one place and he's someplace else.' He glared resentfully towards the trees that housed the sleeping cowboys. 'You'd think someone would have offered to spell me. They're over there snoring their damned heads off while I do all the watching.'

Something was crawling up his arm. Sheriff Purdy cussed and rubbed furiously at the itch. He felt a lump, soft and wet beneath his fingers, and cussed some more. He shifted round to get more comfortable, then stilled as he heard the distinct thud of hoofs. He swivelled towards the sound and peered out past the alfalfa, wanting to call out to his sleeping companions but afraid to make any noise that might alert the horseman.

As the sound drew closer the sheriff was suddenly afraid. An image of the sprawled bodies of the cowboys in the street outside the general store came to his mind. Five of them, and Dillon had gunned them down with nary a scratch to himself. Shaking visibly, the lawman brought up his rifle and eased the hammer back. The first shot would alert the sleepers and they would come to his aid.

He saw a shape at the entrance to the yard and aimed his weapon. Shoot first to be on the safe side. The trouble was the front sight of the rifle kept wavering on and off the target. What if he missed? The killer was a lethal gunman and once alerted he would return fire with deadly accuracy.

The sheriff desperately wanted to empty his bladder. His stomach gurgled so loudly he was frightened the rider would hear it and throw down on him. Sweat beaded his face and dripped in his eyes and he tried blink away the moisture misting his sight. He squinted hard as he tried to concentrate on the horseman.

Let him get closer; then he couldn't miss.

The rider was in the yard walking the horse up to the

burned-out house. Moisture trickled into the lawman's eyes. He blinked rapidly, afraid to let go his rifle to wipe away the sweat and tears. The rifle sight wavered.

Keep steady. Wait till his back is towards you. That way he'll have to turn round to fire. It was an edge.

Fear churned his insides. Lining up the rifle on the figure on top of the big horse, Sheriff Purdy had never been so scared in his life. He had a deadly killer in his sights and he wanted to throw down his rifle and run. The face of Stirling Hornstone suddenly intruded in his thoughts.

'I'm giving you twenty-four hours to bring that son of a bitch in or I'll find someone as will do the job for me.'

There were real tears in Sheriff Purdy's eyes as he squeezed the trigger, the crack of the shot shockingly loud in the quiet morning. Shot after shot he pumped out, hardly able to see through the cloud of gun smoke that hung in the still morning air. His gun empty, Sheriff Purdy collapsed in the field – a trembling wreck of a man, too terrified even to look to see if he had been successful in hitting anything.

There was shouting as the sleeping cowboys awoke and stood up, guns at the ready, looking for the source of the shooting.

'Can you see anything?'

'There's a goddamn horse.'

'Where'd that come from?'

'Careful, the son of a bitch is still out there, somewhere.'

'Where's Purdy?'

'Maybe someone shot the old coot.'

'No loss there then.'

The cowboys were becoming braver now that the shooting seemed to have ceased. They moved in on the yard.

'Holy cow, there's a body here.'

'Hell damnit, all shot to shit.'

'Sheriff Purdy! Where the hell are you?'

The sheriff stood up then. He was still shaking. 'Here,' he called and started walking.

'Was that you shooting?'

He lifted up his rifle showing them. 'Yeah. Did I get the son of a bitch?'

'Sure as shooting you got him all right. He's got more holes than a colander.'

The cowboys were standing round the body. The sheriff couldn't see till he was right up on them. He stared at the bullet-riddled body. His eyes widened.

'Oh, God.'

He turned and was violently sick retching and retching while the cowboys looked on, highly amused.

'Hell, a fella might think he ain't never seen a dead body afore.'

His face like the colour and texture of bread dough, Sheriff Purdy stared with a look of anguish on his face at the bloodied corpse.

'He's just a kid. I didn't know.'

'Who is he anyway?'

Grant Hornstone reached out a boot and flipped the body over.

'Hell, that's the Huger kid. Well done, Sheriff. You hung his pa and now you've shot his kid. We just need to hang his ma and the whole family will be out of our hair.'

Sheriff Purdy staggered back, unable to look at the dead kid any more. He almost keeled over, only someone grabbed his arm.

'I didn't know. The light was bad. I thought it was Dillon. I shouldn't have fired. I shouldn't have shot him. How was I to know?'

No one answered. Grant Hornstone was staring speculatively at the big horse standing nervously by the gate, unwilling to abandon the youngster.

'If I ain't mistaken that's Dillon's horse.' Hornstone was glancing from the dead boy to the horse.

'What is it, boss? You're cooking something up if I ain't mistaken.'

'What I got in mind is a scheme to bring Dillon to us. Go put a halter on that hoss and don't spook it. I got a use for it. For it to work we got to hide this here body. We can bury it. Take a look around and see if you can find a shovel or anything to dig with. Sheriff, you got pencil and paper with you?'

Remorse eating him, Sheriff Purdy nodded, unable to speak.

'I want you to write a note. If that's Dillon's horse, and Yates and me think it is, we attach the note to it and scare it away from here. I reckon it'll go right back to where that son of a bitch is hiding out. Come on, let's get this thing done. I got a good feeling about this. We're going to bait us a trap that will catch us a ring-tailed bobcat.'

24

Amelia heard the hoof beats and squinted into the distance, her hands tightening on the rifle.

'How long do we have to keep hiding out?' she muttered. 'Sure wears a body down and we've only been here a few days.'

She considered waking Dillon, who had bedded down, but decided not to disturb him yet. As far as she could tell it was only one horse. So she waited. The animal came into view trotting up towards the mine. Amelia frowned as she realized there was no rider atop the horse.

On it came until it stopped below her and began to graze. She watched but nothing else happened. She kept peering at the horse. There was something familiar about the animal. When nothing else happened she decided the horse was alone.

Cautiously she climbed down from her lookout position and, as she approached, the horse looked up and came towards her.

'Monday, where on earth did you spring from? I thought you were corralled along with the other horses. What is it, old chap? What has happened? I thought Raoul was looking after you.'

She reached out and patted Monday, then moved round to stand by the saddle. Then she saw the paper tied to the horn with a piece of rawhide. A sense of foreboding swept over her as she reached out and undid the binding. She unfolded the paper and read the note.

'No, oh dear God, no.' Then she was running up the slope. 'Tim , , , Tim. . . .'

He was sitting up when she came upon him, his revolver in his hand. Tearfully she handed him the paper.

'We have your boy,' he read out loud. 'We give Dillon until noon to give himself up. If he don't we'll hang the kid. Sheriff Purdy.'

'They wouldn't,' she said, her voice filled with anguish. 'Surely they wouldn't hurt a child. They're bluffing.'

Dillon shook his head. 'Nah, no one's that bad.'

But he thought otherwise. The cold-blooded murder of his brother and his own brutal treatment at the hands of Hornstone as well as the callous killing of Joe indicated that Raoul was in real danger. Dillon believed Hornstone quite capable of doing what he said in the note.

'What are we going to do? Raoul must be terrified being held by the people who murdered his father.'

She was peering up at him, tears in her eyes. He reached out and she came readily into his arms. Tim held her gently, feeling the softness of her hair on his cheek. He could feel her trembling in his embrace. Tenderly he stroked her hair.

'Don't distress yourself; whatever happens we'll get him back.'

She pulled away looking up at him. 'You know, if you do as they say, once they get their hands on you they'll kill you.'

'Don't you worry what might happen to me. The main concern is to make sure Raoul is safe. Once that's accomplished we'll see what has to be done to keep you and him away from any more harm.'

It was all talk. He knew she was right. He would die in Gainsborough and even that sacrifice would not guarantee the safety of Amelia and her son.

'It's too much to ask of you. I can't let you do it. I'll go myself to Sheriff Purdy and tell him you ran. Ask for my boy and tell them we'll go away from this place. I should have gone when they murdered Ed. But pride kept me here and a desire for vengeance or some sort of justice. I can see now that's not possible. No one can fight Hornstone. He is much too powerful as well as being utterly ruthless. He'll stop at nothing to get his own way.'

She stepped back from him, wiping at her eyes. Dillon felt an overwhelming wave of emotion sweep through him. His heart ached to see her so distressed. And he knew then that he would do anything to protect her and Raoul, even if it meant the ultimate sacrifice.

'Wait,' he said. 'Let us think this thing through. We

both know the vicious nature of these people. There will be no reasoning with them. They have no conscience or feelings of decency or justice. Imagine we are helpless before a mountain lion. Think how you would handle that. You can't parley with a wild beast, but you might be able to lull it into a sense of false security, and when it is off guard, then you strike. With that in mind we must plan a strategy that takes all that into consideration.'

She was watching him uncertainly and he knew his words meant nothing to her. She was a mother and her child was in danger. She could think of nothing else.

'Let's have some coffee while we think this thing over. And while you're making the coffee I'm going into the mine to fetch some of that dynamite. I'm beginning to have the makings of a plan.'

'What about lighting a fire? You said it would give away our hideout.'

'Won't make no difference. I figure they've stopped looking for us for now. They have Raoul and that's their ace in the hole. With that as their bargaining chip they'll be expecting me to turn myself in.'

Over coffee they sat in silence; Amelia fretting about Raoul and what he was going through at the hands of Hornstone, and Dillon mulling over what he had to do to rescue the boy from his captors.

'I need some cotton material that'll make a bandage. Big enough to wrap round my chest and back,' he said at last.

'Your back paining you?'

'A mite, won't do no harm to keep it covered up. Don't want to start bleeding all over Sheriff Purdy when he takes me prisoner.'

'You don't have to do this. We could still try my plan to tell them you've left the territory.'

'Amelia, I've just said, you can't parley with a wild beast. In fact, thinking about it, I'd rather tangle with a bear or a puma as go into that town and hand myself over to Hornstone. Now, if you'd help me with that bandage. I won't be able to do it on my own.'

She stood up and walked into the mine where she had stored some of her belongings, returning shortly with a petticoat and scissors. Dillon stripped his shirt and together they worked on the task. He pulled his shirt back on and then his jacket.

'You wait here and get ready to pull out. I'll send Raoul back to you. I'll put him on Monday and then you two get going away from here. Leave all this sorry mess behind. Start a new life somewhere else. Give Raoul a new start away from the poison that is Hornstone.'

'No.' She was shaking her head. 'I'm not leaving without you.'

'Amelia, don't do this to me.' He put his hands on her shoulders, staring intently into her eyes. 'You got to promise me you'll leave as soon as Raoul is safely back with you.'

'I . . . I . . . '

The anguish showed plainly on her face. He tightened his hold.

'Promise me; promise you'll get the hell out of here. Promise! I can't do this knowing you and Raoul will still be around for Hornstone to hurt you further. I got to be sure you are out of harm's way.'

Her tears were flowing freely now, the struggle almost too much for her.

'I promise,' she sobbed.

She threw her arms around him and kissed him, holding him in a long embrace.

'You come out of this safe, Tim Dillon. And then you

come and find me however long it takes.'

They broke apart. He strode swiftly across to Monday and swung aboard. 'Come back safe,' she called after him, keeping his tall erect figure in sight till he left the gorge.

25

They were waiting for him at the sheriff's office. As soon as they saw him riding in they pulled their weapons. He was surprised how few of them there were. Sheriff Purdy, Grant Hornstone and two other cowboys, all watching as he pulled up outside the jail. He sat his horse, hand on his holstered pistol, not saying anything.

'You're under arrest, Dillon.'

The sheriff looked scared, as if he expected the man on the horse to unlimber his gun and start shooting. Dillon swung down from his horse.

'Release the boy, I want you to put him on this horse and let him ride back to his mother.'

'He's inside,' Hornstone said, 'in a cell. As soon as we got you under lock and key we'll let him go.'

Dillon's eyes narrowed. There was something not quite right here, but he had to go along with them. He stepped up on the boardwalk.

'Take his gun.'

One of the cowboys stepped forward and took Dillon's pistol. They watched him warily as if he would pull some stunt and somehow overcome them all.

'Search him.'

Dillon stood patiently while the cowboy patted him down. For a brief moment the man tugged at the bandage.

'Nothing.'

'Inside.' Hornstone indicated the door with his pistol. 'Any tricks and we'll shoot. But I'd prefer to see you hang.'

They crowded him inside. He didn't see the raised gun as it smashed down on the back of his head. He pitched forward on his knees, his senses swirling.

'The boy . . .' he managed to gasp before he was hit again and sprawled helplessly on the floor.

One on each side they took his arms and dragged him into the cell. He had almost lost consciousness and could do nothing to resist them, desperately trying not to pass out. The cell door clanged behind him. He struggled to his knees, propping himself against the wooden bunk.

'Raoul, you let him go now?'

His voice was tight with suffering; pain was surging in waves through his battered head as he looked up at the gloating face of Grant Hornstone smirking from the other side of the bars.

'Oh, I forgot to tell you. The Huger kid is dead. Sheriff Purdy shot him. Shot that youngster clean off the top of that nag of yours. Thought it was you. But it worked out all right. We used him as bait to lure you right into that there cage where you can't do no more harm.'

Dillon was staring back at his tormentor, his own hurts diminishing as he took in this dire piece of news.

'He was only a kid. . . .'

But then he stopped, realizing it was useless talking with these men. It was as he had told Amelia – it would be like trying to parley with a wild beast. He sank to the floor, his mind a whirl as he considered the consequences of their actions.

Anger flared in him and it was with a real effort he restrained himself from leaping up and venting rage on the iron bars of his cell. Instead he let his shoulders slump and put his head in his hands, the picture of despair as he listened to the conversation of his captors.

'I'm going out to the ranch to tell Pa we have the son of a bitch locked up. I want to be the one to tell him. For once in his life the old bastard is going to be pleased with something I've done.'

'Sure thing, Grant. What you want us to do?'

'Just stay sober and make sure this joker stays locked in that cell. No matter what he wants or says, you ignore him. I'm sure Pa will want to come into town to watch the hanging. It's something I wouldn't want to miss neither. Make sure you tell everybody in town about it. Tell them we want them there to witness what happens to fellas as buck Hornstone. I want to make sure everybody turns out for the hanging. And I mean everyone.'

Hornstone turned back to the cell and sneered in at the prisoner. 'Mister, this is your last day on this earth. Tomorrow morning there's to be a hanging and you're the chief guest. I want you to put on a good show. No choking off early, which gives me an idea.'

He turned back to the sheriff. 'We could hang this galoot and then let loose the noose. Say, that's kind of poetry – loose the noose. That way we could prolong his agony. See how many times we can hang him till he stiffs it. That should provide first-rate fun for the good citizens of Gainsborough.'

'Hell, Grant, that's a darn good idea,' one of the cowboys said and slapped his thigh. 'How's about letting me pull on the rope? I sure would like that.'

'Huh, half the Hornstone crew will be queuing up to haul on that rope. Don't forget we're hanging him for murdering cowpokes as worked with us. The fellas he killed had a lot of friends. They'll all want a hand in the hanging.'

'We could draw lots. Lucky fella gets a spell as hangman.'

'Sure sounds a lot of fun.'

Hornstone turned and grinned at the man slumped in his cell.

'You listening, Dillon? I'm organizing a necktie party for you. It's going to be lots of fun. Folks will bring their kids to watch. I'll make sure you are hauled high enough to be seen by everyone. You'll be the star turn, but I don't want you to get too choked up about it.'

With that parting shot they moved back into the front office. Dillon could hear the voices laughing and joshing as they discussed the impending fate of the prisoner.

The rage he felt gradually cooled to a manageable white hot fury. He took deep breaths trying to gather his strength. The ache in his head lessened to a dull throbbing. As he sat on the floor he was filled with grief for the death of Raoul. It affected him even more than the murder of his own brother, Dexter. He tried to imagine what the news of Raoul's killing would do to Amelia.

'This will surely break her,' he muttered into the empty cell. 'She has lost so much already. We are indeed dealing with wild beasts. In fact beasts are a cut above these savages. They only kill for food or when threatened. Hornstone kills for the sheer pleasure it gives him. He is bereft of any of the finer feelings of civilized humans.'

He was reminded of the obvious pleasure Hornstone and his cowboys took in anticipating the torture and execution of their prisoner.

'Maybe it's time I did a little killing of my own.'

Slowly he pushed himself to his feet, straining to listen

for voices from the outer office, but all seemed quiet. He guessed Hornstone had left for the ranch to tell his father of their success in catching the fugitive and to organize a party to come in town and watch the hanging.

Cautiously he unbuttoned his shirt and slung the garment on the bunk. He unwound the bandage Amelia had bound around his torso, retrieving from among the folds a paper-wrapped cylinder about eight inches long with a short fuse in one end. From his pocket he took the makings and built himself a smoke, thinking of Amelia and how he had sat with her at the campfire and her asking to roll the cigarette for him.

It saddened him to think of that occasion. It had been a little oasis of peace and tranquillity that he believed could never be repeated. Hornstone's brutal actions had seen to that.

'That evil brood poisons everything,' he said as he struck a Lucifer and touched the flame to his smoke.

Leisurely he donned his shirt, took a few more pulls at his cigarette, then walked to the door of the cell. For a moment he listened but could hear nothing that might indicate his jailors might return anytime soon.

He began work in earnest then, upending the bunk, ramming the legs against the rear wall thus making a rectangular refuge. He retrieved the homemade bandage and used it to secure the stick of dynamite to the cell door, wrapping it around the lock and using all the material so that he finished with a substantial lump. He touched his cigarette to the fuse, climbed into the narrow space behind the bed and pulled the straw mattress over him.

26

Even though he had his ears plugged with cotton the explosion set Dillon's head ringing and amplified the pain in his battered skull. Something pinged into the wall above him and the bed behind which he was sheltering lifted up a few inches, then dropped back again. It took a real effort of will to throw the protective mattress from him and clamber out from his shelter.

Using the mattress to cushion the impact he slammed his shoulder into the door. The resulting shock to his body set surges of pain echoing through his pistol-whipped head. It took two goes and a resurgence of an agonizing headache before the door crashed open. Then he was plunging out into the front office.

Sheriff Purdy was standing up from his chair behind the desk blinking owlishly as if he had just been jolted out of sleep; in fact he had been trying to catch up on a night's lost shuteye when he had stayed awake to trap the fugitives in the expectation that they might come back to the burnt-out ranch.

Dillon was across the office in a couple of strides and dived over the desk, his fist smashing into the sheriff's face. The lawman went backwards and crashed to the floor, tangled up in his chair. Dillon hit him again for good measure. Dazed and confused by the swift turn of events, Sheriff Purdy was unable to protect himself from the whirlwind attack.

The sheriff's gunbelt was hanging on a peg. Dillon

grabbed it quickly and slung the looped belt across his shoulder. He aimed the gun at the sheriff's face.

'You murdering son of a bitch. I ought to put a bullet in you for killing an innocent boy, but I still have some use for you. On your feet, you piece of slime.'

Blubbering in terror, Sheriff Purdy struggled upright. At that moment the front door crashed open and one of Hornstone's cowboys burst in, waving his gun.

'What the hell was that?' he managed to shout, then he spotted Dillon.

'Throw your gun down!' Dillon roared.

Even as he shouted he guessed it was a lost cause. The cowhand's gun swung towards him, but Dillon fired first, putting two slugs into the ranny's chest. The man's mouth opened as if in protest, but the bullets punched him back out through the doorway. Dillon jammed his pistol into the terrified sheriff's ear.

'Move.' Shoving the lawman towards the door. 'What have you done with my horse?'

'The livery, we took it down the livery.'

Dillon pushed the lawman out through the door and immediately gunfire erupted.

'Hell. . . '

Sheriff Purdy staggered back, crashing into Dillon who was but a step behind. Dillon glimpsed the Hornstone cowboy in the street, his smoking gun in his hand. Before the sheriff could fall Dillon propelled him roughly through the doorway. More shots rang out and the sheriff crumpled to the ground.

Dillon leapfrogged the body, firing as his feet hit the boardwalk. He saw the cowboy stagger back and fall to the ground as his bullets hit home. Quickly he scanned the street but no one else was in sight. He took off running, his eyes darting around, alert for further trouble. Nothing occurred to distract him from his purpose of getting to the livery.

Quickly he found his tackle and saddled up, then he led Monday to the doorway. Cautiously he peered outside, scanning the street and buildings, but the place appeared deserted.

Dillon began to wonder if the two cowboys were the extent of Hornstone's force left to guard the jail. He recalled there had been only Hornstone, Sheriff Purdy and the two gunmen to greet him when he came into town to surrender. Hornstone had left for the ranch to bring the news of Dillon's capture and fetch his pa into Gainsborough to watch the hanging he had arranged, leaving Sheriff Purdy and the two gunnies to watch over him. With Dillon safely behind bars Hornstone would reckon his prisoner was secure until he returned.

Dillon mounted and rode along the deserted street, passing the jail with the three bodies, like discarded scraps of humanity, lying where they had fallen.

'Might be a goddamn ghost town for all the life about it,' he muttered.

But it did not stop him checking likely places that might conceal lurking gunmen as he rode from the town. Once clear of the buildings Dillon still did not urge Monday into a faster pace. He was thinking of the task that lay ahead of him.

'Goddamn it, I'd rather face a howling band of Apaches than have to face Amelia right now,' he growled. 'How am I going to tell her about Raoul?' But even as he said it he realized the selfishness of his behaviour. 'Gee up there, Monday. I just have to get back and break the bad news to her.'

She was frowning as he rode up, wondering how he had managed to return so quickly and wondering why Raoul was not with him.

'Something's wrong,' she exclaimed. 'Where's Raoul?' Her eyes were deep pools of apprehension.

Dillon stepped down from the horse, allowing the reins to drop to the dirt, staring at her, unable to voice the unspeakable.

'No . . .' her face collapsed in a spasm of alarm. 'Raoul, what has happened to my Raoul?'

He stepped close, wanting to comfort her, but she backed away from him.

'What happened?'

'I'm sorry, Amelia, they killed him.' Not knowing how else to tell her.

Her howl of anguish drove like a knife into his heart. He tried to reach her again but she kept stepping back.

'Tell me it's not true! My boy, my boy; oh my poor Raoul.'

He was helpless before her grief, his own face a tragic mask. 'I'm sorry, Amelia.' He was aching to take her in his arms and comfort her.

She raised her face to the sky and howled like a wounded animal.

'My poor boy, ah, Raoul, what have they done to you?'

Her shoulders slumped and she stood there sobbing. Slowly he moved closer.

'Amelia.'

She looked at him but he could see the blankness in her eyes. This time when he reached out for her she did not resist. He held her, listening to her weeping into his shirt, feeling her body trembling, and he could not help his own tears, keeping her close till her sobs became a whimper.

'Take me to him. I must see him.'

'I don't know what they've done with him. I was think-ing he probably went back to the house. They must have got him there. We can go and look.'

Dumbly she nodded.

'Wait here; I'll go down and fetch a pony for you.'

'No, I'll come with you.'

They walked in silence to the little corral Raoul had constructed to pen the horses. The kid had used lariats salvaged from the cow ponies. Tim saddled up one of the mounts for Amelia and they set out for her burnt-out home, not sure what they would find when they got there.

27

At the abandoned homestead they wandered around the site searching until Dillon discovered the disturbed earth. He told her to go and secure the horses while he uncovered the grave. His heart was heavy with grief as he lifted the small body, thinking how light it was.

He laid his burden in the grass and Amelia came and knelt beside it, wiping with her fingers at the dirt that had adhered to the boy's face. Her tears dripped in a constant stream as she worked.

'I'll need water,' she said dully, looking around. 'I'll need to wash him.'

Together they laid him out and cleaned him as best they could with grasses soaked in water along with Amelia's tears. When they had done what they could, Dillon removed his saddle blanket and wrapped the body in it.

'We should take him into Gainsborough to be buried with his father,' she said.

'The town will be crawling with Hornstone's people. I had to shoot my way out of there. It was Sheriff Purdy as killed him. They claimed he thought it was me on top of Monday. If it's any comfort the sheriff is dead. One of Hornstone's men shot him when trying to get me. If we bury him here for now maybe at a later date we can take him into the cemetery.'

He dug a fresh grave near the house in what had been the garden.

'You want me to say a few words?' he asked.

He had been at many a graveside and had a fair idea what to say. She nodded, her eyes black holes in her pale face.

'Today, Lord, we give into your care an innocent young boy who hardly had time to make his mark in this life. I know he has his daddy there on the other side to greet him and comfort him. Ed and Raoul Huger are in your care now. You take good care of them, you hear, Lord. They were both good folks who did not deserve the hand they were dealt in this life. I know their lot will be better in their new existence. Amen.'

Tears were streaming down Amelia's face. Dillon moved to her side and put a comforting arm around her. They stood together, not saying anything, enduring the heavy burden of grief.

'The hunt will really be on for us now,' he said eventually. 'They've tried to kill me three times and failed and I've been responsible for several of their men being killed or injured, as well as their sheriff. They had me in jail and were fixing to hang me. From now on I imagine their orders will be to shoot on sight. We won't be safe staying in one place any more. We have get you away to a place of safety. I'm sorry to have brought all this trouble on you.'

She turned to him and stared hard into his eyes.

'Don't you apologize for things that were not of your doing. It is as you said; we are dealing with wild dogs. It is they who brought this misery down upon me.' She paused, her eyes locked on his. 'Once you have taken me to a place of sanctuary what then?'

He looked away before answering. 'I guess I'll keep on riding.'

'Don't lie to me, Tim Dillon. I have known you for only a matter of days and yet I know you are not the sort of man to turn tail and run. I want to stay and fight alongside you.'

'It'll be hellish dangerous. I—'

'You think I can ride away from here with my son and my husband in the ground,' she interrupted him. 'I have as much right to fight Hornstone as you. I'll not be a burden. I can shoot and I can ride. Just tell me what I have to do.'

There was a long pause before he spoke. 'So be it. Neither of us might survive but at least we will have caused Hornstone a few headaches.'

Back at the mine they quickly gathered their belongings and distributed the baggage among the cow ponies. There was no talking as they went about their tasks. Dillon filled a saddlebag with dynamite.

Once more they set out to find a new hideout. They had travelled only a few miles before finding a tree-dotted knoll that had a good all-round view of the approaches. Once more Dillon corralled the horses at a site separate from the main camp.

During these activities they did not talk much. Dillon had formed a plan to strike a blow against Hornstone which required him to be away from the camp to accomplish it, but he was very aware of Amelia, sunk in her grief, and he worried about leaving her alone.

'I won't be gone long,' he told her. 'There are things I need to collect. Will you be all right on your own?'

'Don't worry about me.' For a moment he thought she was going to break down but she recovered. 'Any of Hornstone's men comes sneaking round here and I'm firing no more warning shots. Any reservations I might have had about killing snakes are well and truly crushed.'

As it was he was gone for only a short time. Amelia watched him ride in before stepping out from her place of concealment behind a large oak. She watched as he swung down from Monday, puzzled by the horned skulls dangling from his saddle.

'You been out collecting skulls?'

'Yep, I have a little scheme which I will reveal presently. I told you I stampeded a herd of longhorns through the Hornstone ranch. With a bit of luck they should have flattened everything in their path, including the barbed wire fence guarding the house and outbuildings.'

Dillon smiled across at her, thinking she seemed to have recovered somewhat from her grief, but there were dark smudges beneath her eyes and she did not return his smile. He untied the macabre trophies and slung them to the ground. There were four skulls still with horns attached.

'We used to employ Indian scouts back in my army days. They taught me how to make a bow and this is the raw material for the job.'

'What need do you have for a bow? I thought we had plenty of guns.'

'There'll be no respite while Hornstone is hunting us. The reason I was able to stampede his cattle was that he had the most of his hands out hunting me. When I went for those longhorns there were only a couple of cowboys riding herd. I imagine there would normally be a lot more tending the cattle but Hornstone had taken them out to help track us down. If it worked out right those longhorns should have stampeded right through his ranch and trampled everything in their path, including the fence. Now Hornstone has the problem of rounding them up. I doubt if he can spare too many men to go hunting for us for the next few days. With that in mind we can stay here while I make my bow and tell you how I intend to use it.'

He set her to soaking strips of rawhide while he worked on the horns, first cutting them free and disposing of the skulls. With his knife he hollowed out the thick end of one horn and jammed the pointed end of another inside. He did this till he had the horns joined in a couple of curves. Using the treated rawhide he bound the joints tightly and finally whittled a wooden handle which he attached by the same method to the middle of his creation. As he worked he told her his plan.

'Like I say, if I am right, the fencing around the ranch will be destroyed. I plan to sneak in there with this trusty weapon strapped to my back.' Dillon hefted his partly finished bow. 'I shall then shoot arrows with dynamite attached into the ranch. It is in retaliation for burning down your home.'

'You can't do it. It'll be far too dangerous. Surely they'll have guards patrolling.'

He stared grimly at her, but then carried on working on his primitive weapon.

'That's why I need the bow. It is silent, and in the dark I can sneak in close, do my work and sneak out again. Do you think you can cut some of the spare harness we have from those Hornstone cow ponies and make me a quiver?'

They worked steadily till there was not enough light to

see. At the end of their labours he had a serviceable bow and several arrows which he fletched with bark, peeled from a tree. He made a few practice shots and his arrows bounced from the tree trunks he was aiming at. Dillon was more than satisfied. He slid the arrows into the makeshift quiver that Amelia had fashioned.

'Squaw, I have heap plenty bow. I go hunt buffalo. We have feast when I return.'

In the gloom he could not tell if his attempt at humour was successful but at least he had made the effort to lessen her anxiety. They had a cold supper of beans and jerky washed down with water from a nearby stream.

'Hopefully we'll have a quiet night, but we can't afford to let our guard down. We'll take turns to stand watch.'

'I'll go first,' she said. 'Last time we did this I suspect you did both mine and Raoul's stint.'

It was as he'd hoped, the night was quiet and they were not disturbed. In the morning she asked him when he proposed to make his attack on Hornstone.

'All being well, I'll go tonight. Have everything packed and ready to go for when I return. We'll move on and find a fresh camp. After tonight's raid the hunt for us will intensify. We'll have to keep on the move.'

28

Rage still simmered in Stirling Hornstone from when his useless son had taken him into Gainsborough to witness the hanging of the man who had killed several of his cowhands. Instead they had found Sheriff Purdy dead along with the two gunhands who had been set to look after the prisoner. It had taken all his control not to beat his son to death when the day's disasters had been revealed.

'You had the critter in jail and you let him escape. Not only that, he's killed Purdy and two more hands. That son of a bitch is laughing at us while he runs rings around you. All you managed to do is to kill a cub and then let a rattler escape.

'You say this son of a bitch could be anywhere. We need a tracker. Someone as can stalk that bastard and lead you to him. Toby Mossman, as lives in a shack on Possum Rise. I know the son of a bitch takes the odd steer from us now and then but I leave him alone, for he hunts big cats and keeps them from bothering my cattle. I reckon he owes me. Send someone over there. Tell him what's required. Maybe offer him a reward.'

Mossman had come, eager to earn the bounty offered by Hornstone.

'Tell me all you know about this fella Dillon. What's his background and what all he's done since coming here.'

Toby Mossman was an old buffalo and Indian hunter. His face looked like someone had stretched jerky across the front of his skull. He was scarred and gnarled like the old buffalo bulls he had helped hunt to extinction.

Grant Hornstone was uncomfortable in the company of the man, thinking he smelt like one of the animals he had once hunted.

'Army fella – was a captain in the cavalry. Took up with a widow woman whose husband was hanged for rustling. Then came into Gainsborough and gunned down five of our cowhands. We had him in prison but he escaped, killed the sheriff and two of his deputies. Stampeded a herd of longhorns right through the ranch. He's hiding out in the hills somewhere with the woman. We got to catch him afore he causes more mischief. You think you can find him?'

Mossman was chewing tobacco and spat a long string of juice before he replied.

'Ain't a man alive I can't track.'

'I got twenty men to help us.'

'Nah, too many. You, me and two others.'

'Hell, this is a dangerous owlhoot. He's killed more than a score of our hands, including Sheriff Purdy.'

'Don't make no difference. A whole pile of riders blundering about will scare him off. Hunting's all about softly, softly.'

'Goddamn it! I don't like it one little bit. This Dillon is as wily as a hound dog with a pilfered steak.'

Argue as he might, Mossman was adamant and the hunt began with Grant Hornstone and just two of his gunhands.

'We start from the widow's place.'

As they approached the burnt-out ranch Mossman stopped.

'Wait here. I'll go in alone. Don't want you tramping all over the place and wiping out sign.'

They watched from afar as the hunter dismounted and spent some time wandering around the site. Hornstone fumed and fretted at the delay. Eventually Mossman waved them in.

'Someone was killed here. I found a fresh grave. You know anything about that?'

'Hell, Sheriff Purdy shot the Huger boy. Reckoned he mistook him for Dillon.'

'There's a lot of tracks coming and going. I think I can make out the most recent going from here. While I got my eyes on the ground looking for sign I want you and your boys watching out for anything suspicious. Seeing as this *hombre* is so cunning I don't want to ride into an ambush. You hear me. Keep your eyes peeled.'

Slowly the tracker rode ahead, scanning the ground and finding enough sign to follow. It was late in the afternoon when they reached the abandoned mine.

'They were here. Spent a few days. Then moved on again not so long ago. Maybe yesterday or day afore.' Mossman looked at the sky. 'Daylight's going but we'll keep tracking. They mightn't have moved far. This fella is wise to hiding out. Ain't seen no sign of no fires. From now on we move cautious. No talking or any kind of noise. We don't know how far they've gone.'

Their progress was slower now and darkness settled in without their sighting the fugitives.

'We'll make camp here,' the tracker announced. 'Can't track in the dark.'

The cowboys were glad of the break from the monotonous drag of slow riding.

'Charlie, see if you can find wood to make a fire,' Grant ordered.

'No fire,' Mossman ordered.

'What the hell you mean?' snarled Hornstone. 'We've been riding all day. We need a shot of java.'

'Why do you think the fella we're tracking don't have no fires? Hell, I could ride up to his camp if he would only light up and send me a signal as to where he is.'

With much grumbling the men agreed to settle down for the night without the comfort of a fire. For supper they had to make do with chewing jerky washed down with water.

As darkness deepened Mossman appeared restless and kept getting up and staring into the night.

'I get the feeling our quarry ain't that far away. He's somewhere out there. Maybe even knows we're following him. I got to follow my instincts. I'm going to cast around a mite, see if I can't find something. You fellas stay here, but try and keep alert. If this fella is as sneaky as you say he could well creep in here and slit all your throats. Then where would I be, all alone out here with no brave cowboys to protect me.'

They heard him chuckling as he faded into the night.

'Son of a bitch,' snarled Hornstone. 'That smelly piece of buffalo dung ain't got no respect for me. When this is all over I'm going to pistol-whip that piece of buffalo shit.'

The object of this rancour moved out through the trees. Mossman was as comfortable moving about at night as he was during the day. He could have carried on tracking with his companions, but he knew their blundering about in the dark would probably alert their quarry. His hunter's instincts were telling him the people he hunted were not that far ahead of them.

Stealthily he moved through the night, stepping lightly, his senses alert, listening and sniffing the air for anything that might indicate human activity. He was walking a long time before he stopped and decided to return to his surly companions. Then he heard the faint noise that could have been anything, but the hunter's keen ears distinguished it from all the other night sounds.

It was a horse moving somewhere out on his right. He stood immobile, listening as the sound faded. Now he had a bearing and he attempted to trace the sound backwards, moving noiselessly through the night like a shadow.

It was a horse again that helped him in his search. Not one horse but several. At first he could smell the animals, then, as he tracked towards them, he could hear them. He had found the fugitives but wondered if they had left on some errand. There had been only one horse on the move and yet Hornstone had told him there were two people to be found – the man Dillon, and the woman.

Slowly he quartered back and forth. It did not take him long to find the horses. Cautiously he watched and listened but could detect no humans. His respect for the fugitive grew. Keeping the mounts separate from the camp was good practice. It meant that in an emergency a man had a chance to evade his pursuers, get to his horse and make a getaway.

After that it was easy to find the camp. Unobserved he watched the woman. She was restless and moved around tidying and fussing at things. It did not take him long to realize she was on her own. Silently he moved in.

29

Even though it was dark as Dillon approached Hornstone he could make out the devastation caused by the stampeding cattle. No fences were standing, which was one of the things he had hoped to achieve so that he could move in on the property and retreat unhindered by barbed wire. Except for the sounds of beasts corralled in the various pens the ranch was quiet. A few lights showed here and there at windows but there seemed to be a general lack of activity. Dillon supposed most of the cowboys were either out hunting him or chasing the stampeded cattle.

He sat on his horse watching the place, then faded back as he heard a horse approach. He watched a rider as he patrolled around the perimeter. He settled down to wait in order to time how long it took the guard to return. It was a good half- hour before the rider appeared again. Dillon ground-hitched Monday and crept forward, his bow at the ready with his quiver of arrows slung across his shoulder.

When he judged the distance to be about right he took out three arrows one by one and laid them on the grass. He had prepared the missiles back at camp. Each arrow had a stick of dynamite bound to the shaft with a short length of fuse jutting from one end. Shielding the match in his fist he lit a cigarette and took a few pulls till he got it glowing brightly. Using the smouldering cigarette he lit the first fuse and fitted the deadly arrow to his bow.

The arrow arced into the air towards the ranch house. He repeated the process with the other two, not sure where his missiles were landing. The darkness and the primitive bow hindered accurate shooting. It did not matter. The resulting explosions should unnerve Hornstone and keep him and his cowhands rattled.

His mission accomplished Dillon quickly withdrew, clambered aboard Monday and rode quietly away. All the time he was listening for the explosions of the bombs he had deposited on or near the house.

The first detonation echoed through the night. Dillon smiled with satisfaction as two more explosions ripped the quiet of the evening apart. He had hoped to pay back Hornstone for the burning of Amelia's home and maybe injure or kill the rancher in justified retribution for the murder of her son and her husband. Satisfied with the night's work, he set a steady pace back to the hills pondering his next move.

Tonight's raid on Hornstone would have been a mighty

blow struck against the formidable rancher; one that he might find difficult to recover from. Dillon's campaign of terror was designed to wear his enemy down; striking one blow after another and letting everyone see that Hornstone was not such a power that he couldn't be brought low.

Cautiously he approached their new campsite. When he could view it he halted and cast an eye over the place. He saw where Amelia had wrapped herself up in her blankets and frowned. They had both agreed a watch must be maintained at all times.

'Hell, the poor gal is exhausted after all she has gone through.'

But it worried him all the same. The people hunting them had proved time and time again how ruthless they were. He and Amelia could not afford to let their guard down. He dismounted, leaned his bow and quiver of arrows against a tree, then removed the saddle. Knowing Monday would not stray far, he gave the horse a reassuring pat on the rump and walked into the camp, trying to be quiet in order not to disturb the sleeping woman.

It soon became apparent he had not been that quiet, for Amelia stirred from under the blankets and sat up. Only it wasn't Amelia but Grant Hornstone. He had a .45 in his hand and the weapon was pointed at Dillon.

'Howdy, Dillon, nice of you to turn up. You keep late hours. Wonder what mischief you were up to tonight?'

Dillon made a move for his holstered gun but stopped when a new voice from the side spoke.

'Dillon, we got your woman with a gun at her head. You make any wrong moves and she'll be the first to die. Then we'll cut you down.'

He stopped moving – waiting. There was nothing he could do. They had him cold.

'Undo your gunbelt and let it slide to the dirt.'

By now Hornstone had clambered to his feet, smirking all over his face and keeping his Colt aimed at Dillon.

'Don't harm the woman. She has nothing to do with this. Just let her go. I'm the one you're after.'

'Uh-uh, she's guilty of aiding a renowned killer. Now do as you're told and shuck that gun.'

There was nothing Dillon could do. He was well and truly trapped. Any hostile move on his part would surely result in Amelia's death. He undid his belt and held it out.

'Drop it in the dirt.'

'I need to know if Mrs Huger is unharmed. For all I know you could have killed her already.'

'Mossman, bring her out in the open.'

Dillon watched as Amelia was marched from cover. A gun was pressed against her head and she had been gagged with a bandanna which was why she had been unable to call out a warning. His shoulders sagged and he dropped the gun rig.

'Move away from the gun.'

'Can't you take that gag off her? She doesn't deserve being treated like that.'

'Just do as you're told and we'll think about it.'

As Dillon moved to comply with Hornstone's instructions, two more figures moved out from the trees. They both held guns and had them lined up on Dillon.

'Hold him.'

The cowboys holstered their weapons and came each side of Dillon. They grabbed an arm apiece. Only when he was secured did Hornstone come close. He too holstered his weapon, then he drew back his fist and punched hard into the captive's midriff. Dillon's breath went from him and he doubled over. The cowboys pulled him upright. Again and again Hornstone punched, leaving his victim hanging weakly between the cowboys. Dillon was gagging, trying to suck in air – his ribs and midriff hurting with every movement.

'You son of a bitch, you caused us a lot of grief, but no more. You've already escaped one hanging. We won't make that mistake again.'

Hornstone drew his pistol and for a moment Dillon thought he was about to be shot. He peered at the rancher through pain-dimmed eyes, wishing he had just a couple of minutes alone with the man before he died.

'Go to hell,' was all he could manage.

'That's where you're going, my friend. Very shortly you'll be toasting your feet at Satan's fireside. Fetch his horse and a rope. I'll keep him covered.'

One of the cowboys let go his arm and Dillon sagged to his knees, the remaining cowboy being unable to support his weight. The second cowboy let go and moved to one side drawing his pistol and keeping it aimed at the captive. Dillon knelt in the dirt, bent over, waves of pain coursing through this battered body.

'We're going to hang you, Dillon. I ain't going to take you back to town this time. Three times you've escaped death. I ain't taking no chances on you breaking loose again. This time your luck has run out.'

'Get him on the horse and put that noose around his neck.'

The cowboys struggled to hoist Dillon on top of Monday. He didn't make it easy, allowing his body to loll about helplessly.

'Son of a bitch, he weighs as much as a goddamned steer,' one of the cowboys complained.

At last they had the condemned man in position. Hornstone stepped up beside Monday so he could look up at his victim.

'I killed your no-good cheating brother, Dillon. Didn't

want you to go out of this world not knowing. He wouldn't tell us where he stashed the money he stole from me. So I beat him. In the end I got angry with that stubborn son of a bitch and I shot him. Bang! Just like that. We searched his room and found the money hid in the fireplace. He could have saved himself a lot of grief.'

Dillon was slumped on top of the horse peering out of the corner of his eye at his tormentor, not responding.

'You hear me, Dillon? I shot that son of a bitch of a brother of yours.' Hornstone was getting riled up because he was getting no obvious reaction from his captive. 'And you know what; we're all going to have our turn with your woman afore hanging her.'

He turned and looked over his shoulder at Amelia. 'You hear me, Amelia? You had your chance to be my woman but you thought yourself too high and mighty for the likes of me. I went to a lot of trouble over you. Even had your husband hanged so as you'd be free. Yes, that's how bad I wanted you. Now I get to have you on my terms.' Hornstone sniggered. 'I just hope you're worth it.'

One of the cowboys sought out a suitable branch and expertly tossed the rope over it while Hornstone and his companion kept their guns on the captive.

'Get that noose around his neck. Say your prayers, you son of a bitch. It's the end of the trail for you.'

30

Dillon muttered the command he used when he needed Monday to collapse in the dirt and lie flat so that rider and horse became an unobtrusive bump hidden in the long grass. It had been a useful trick that had got Dillon out of tight spots in the past. The horse obediently went down, knocking into Hornstone.

Hornstone screamed as a ton of horseflesh collapsed on him. At the same time Dillon launched himself on top of his tormentor. Trapped beneath Monday the rancher could make no resistance as Dillon crashed into him and wrested the pistol from his unresisting hand.

Mossman was so engrossed watching the preparations for the hanging that he had stepped forward, his pistol no longer jammed in Amelia's face. From his prone position Dillon put two slugs into the hunter's chest. Mossman staggered back, blood blossoming from his shirt front.

Dillon rolled to one side and a bullet buried itself in the dirt where he had been lying. He crouched behind Hornstone, who was writhing about in agony and screaming.

The two cowboys were trying to shoot Dillon but firing wide for fear of hitting their boss. Partly sheltered by Hornstone and by Monday's bulk, Dillon had no such inhibitions. He fired steadily and deliberately. The range was short. No more than yards separated him from his targets. One man went down with a slug in his belly. His companion turned to run and, taking aim, Dillon put a bullet in the back of his head. The man pitched forward and Dillon was looking round for more targets but it seemed he had eliminated the opposition.

Beside him Hornstone was reduced to moaning and begging someone to help him. Dillon ignored the weeping man and, getting painfully to his feet, stumbled across to Amelia. As well as being gagged her hands had been tied with rawhide. He tackled the gag first.

'Oh, Tim, I'm so sorry. I should have kept better watch.'

'Hush now, you ain't got nothing to apologize for.'

He had to search the dead hunter for a knife to sever the rawhide binding her wrists. As soon as she was free she threw her arms around him and held him tight. He winced as she squeezed his bruised body. When at last she released him she looked around at the bodies littering the campsite.

'You killed them all.'

'Hornstone's still alive, more's the pity. Are you all right? Did they hurt you?'

'Hornstone slapped me around some but the smelly one made him stop. He said he was afraid you would return and catch them before they could lay their ambush for you.'

Dillon turned and looked across at the trapped Hornstone, who was now weeping piteously.

'He is a loathsome creature. I'm tempted to put him out of his misery with a bullet, but we may be able to use him to our own advantage.'

Dillon called to Monday and the horse obediently rose to its feet. Alternately weeping and moaning Hornstone stayed where he was, his legs so badly crushed he was unable to stand.

'Help me. For God's sake help me.'

Dillon was looking thoughtfully at the weeping man.

'Have we got any paper?' he asked Amelia.

'Yes, I have some from when I was teaching Raoul to write.' Her eyes welled up with tears as she was reminded of her murdered son. 'Why do you ask?'

'You heard Hornstone confess to those murders; I figure we ought to write it all out and make him sign it. That way when we get it to a judge he'll pay the price for his crimes.' He leaned forward and whispered in her ear. 'Make two copies.'

While Amelia got to work on the confession Dillon hunkered down beside his enemy.

'You're at our mercy, Hornstone. I'm not sure why I don't just finish you off and ride out of here. Or better still leave you here for the buzzards to do the job for me. But I'm giving you a chance to save yourself.'

'I'll do anything you want,' Hornstone wailed. 'Just get me to a doctor.'

'We're writing out your confession. I want you to sign it. Then I'll get you on a horse and take you into Gainsborough.'

'Yes, yes. I'll sign anything – anything!'

They propped him up while he moaned and wept at the pain in his crushed limbs. He signed the confession without protest, admitting to the murders of Edward Huger, Dexter Dillon, Joe Briggs, and accessory to the murder of Raoul Huger.

'How are we going to transport him?' Amelia asked. 'He can't sit a horse like that.'

'We'll have to use your cart. One of us will go back to the mine and bring that back. We load him on that and take him into Gainsborough.'

Hornstone passed out as they were manhandling him into the cart. Dillon was none too gentle during the operation, his own hurts making him careless of the discomfort he was causing Hornstone as he and Amelia hauled the injured man on to the wagon. Hornstone was wearing a sheepskin jacket. After studying the man for a moment Dillon took out the knife he had used to cut Amelia's bonds and slit a hole in the lining of the jacket. He inserted a stick of dynamite threading the end of the fuse up through the material and out underneath the collar. Amelia's eyes widened when she realized what he had done.

'Do you intend to blow him up?'

'Nah, just a mite of insurance. The Hornstones are a treacherous breed. A fella needs to keep one step ahead when dealing with such deadly creatures.'

They left the bodies of the hunter and the two cowboys where they lay.

'Let Hornstone senior recover the bodies if he is so inclined, which I doubt somehow. I don't feel up to hauling any more dead weight about. That pounding Hornstone gave me shook me up a mite.'

'It was horrible. I had to watch him do it to you and I couldn't do a thing about it. It's all my fault. If they hadn't caught me then you needn't have gone through all that.'

'Amelia, how many times have I got to tell you? You're not to blame for any of this. If anyone is to blame it's me. I came busting in on the Hornstones and stirred them up. You saved my life when Joe fetched me to your place. I owe you a life. So don't you go reproaching yourself any. You hear me?'

She smiled at him and at that moment Dillon felt he could have gone into Hornstone's ranch and taken on the whole mob of cowboys singlehanded.

'Come on,' he said, 'let's get this thing over with.'

The journey to Gainsborough was uneventful. As they entered the town some folk, recognizing them, came out on the boardwalks to observe the group: Amelia driving the cart with the injured Hornstone and Dillon riding Monday.

They pulled up outside the Bottom Dollar. Dillon dismounted and went inside. The barkeep stared with disbelief as Dillon sauntered up to the bar. His hand slid beneath the counter.

'You pull a weapon and you're a dead man, Waters,' Dillon snapped. 'Put your hands where I can see them.' The barkeep did as he was told, glaring sourly at his visitor. 'Your good friend, Grant Hornstone is outside with his legs busted. A horse fell on him accidental and he's in a bad way. I need a couple of hands to carry him inside. Then someone fetch the sawbones.'

Waters gaped at him. 'Mr Hornstone hurt, you say, and you brought him here?'

'In spite of what people say about me I'm really a kind-hearted sort of fella. Now are you going to organize that help or are you going to wait till Hornstone dies out in the street?'

While the process of moving the injured man was going on Dillon heard a horse gallop out of town. He figured a messenger was being sent to Hornstone. He expected the rancher would come storming into town with a mass of guns to back him. He took Amelia to one side.

'I want you to take Monday and ride hell for leather for Preston. Take Hornstone's signed confession to the local law office. Tell whoever's in charge all that has happened here.'

'I can't just leave you. We'll both go.'

'That won't work. As soon as Hornstone learns we've fled he'll have people after us. I have to remain to keep his attention focused here.'

'They'll kill you.'

148

'Nah, I'll have Grant under my gun. We'll negotiate some kind of agreement.'

There were more arguments mixed in with tears, but in the end Amelia agreed to do as she was told.

'I'll be fine,' he assured her as he helped her aboard Monday. 'When we meet again all this will be settled.'

But Dillon wasn't sure if he would be alive come morning.

31

The thunder of hoofs vibrated through the town and drove people off the streets. Everyone knew what it meant. Stirling Hornstone pulled up outside the Bottom Dollar, his riders filling the street. A nod of his head and half a dozen gunnies dismounted and entered the saloon. They found their quarry inside.

Dillon was sitting quietly beside Grant Hornstone who was propped up in a chair with his bandaged legs resting on a second chair. Dillon was smoking a large cigar and holding a Colt with the muzzle casually pointed at his captive.

'It's about time you fellas turned up,' snarled the injured man. 'I could have been dead and buried in the time it took you to get here.'

The gunmen said nothing, spreading out so they hemmed in the man sitting beside Grant. One of them returned to the front door.

'All secure here, boss. We got the son of a bitch covered.'

Stirling Hornstone strode into the saloon, his gaze taking in the situation. He strode over and stood looking down at the man guarding his son.

'You caused me a lot of grief fella. It ends today.'

'That's what I was hoping. We come to an amiable agreement and your son, Grant here, survives and I get to ride out of here without the danger of your men gunning me down.'

For long moments Hornstone studied the man guarding his son.

'You've caused me a lot of trouble. You shoot up a passel of my men. You stampede my own cattle through my ranch. Cause me to lose hundreds of working hours because my men are out hunting you instead of punching cattle which is what I pay them for. I guess it was you as bombed my house. You think I can let you walk away after all that?'

Dillon shrugged. 'It's either that or I put a bullet in Grant. I'm bargaining his life for mine. I know if it comes to a fight I'm outgunned. One man against – how many did you bring – probably thirty or forty armed men. On the plus side, just consider this; I brought Grant in so the sawbones could treat him. I could have left him to die out in the hills. I must tell you I was tempted to do just that. If you want to bury the rest of his little party Grant can tell you where the bodies are.'

'You killed Mossman?'

'I wasn't introduced, but if he was a rancid old goat that smelt like he hadn't had a bath in a coon's age that would probably be him. He's out there with two other fellas.'

Hornstone's eyes narrowed. 'I'm counting you've killed more than a score of my cowboys. You also murdered

Sheriff Purdy.'

'I didn't keep tally. They keep coming I keep knocking them down.'

'They tell me you were a cavalry captain. I guess that's where you learned your fighting.'

'I guess. Now enough of the civilities. We agree a deal: you get your son's life and I get ride out of here unmolested.'

Hornstone shrugged his shoulders. 'I guess, but I want your gun. I don't want you doing any more killing.'

'You get my gun when I have your word I have safe passage out of Gainsborough.'

The rancher nodded. 'You got it.'

'Say it; I want you to say it in front of witnesses.'

'Goddamn it, yes. I swear you can ride out of here if you give up your gun.'

Dillon looked down at the Colt. 'You hear that, Grant? Even though you killed my brother I'm calling it quits. No more killing.'

'You son of a bitch, I ain't swearing nothing. As soon as I can ride again I'm coming after you.'

Dillon nodded. 'I thought you would say something like that.'

He turned and held out the Colt towards Stirling Hornstone. The ranch boss nodded to one of his gunnies. The man moved up and took the weapon.

'Wait, Pa, he has a confession – about me killing his brother and all.'

The rancher was watching Dillon carefully. 'That true?'

Dillon scowled. 'Hell, I just wanted it for surety. I have a feeling it mightn't stand up in court.'

'You got it on you?'

For a moment it looked as if Dillon was going to refuse; then he shrugged, pulled out the crumpled paper and tossed it on Grant's lap. The hand with the cigar was resting on the back rail of the wounded man's chair.

'Take him, boys. Get him outside and string him up,' Stirling Hornstone snarled.

Dillon stared at the rancher as his men moved in. 'You swore in front of all these people. I was to have safe passage.'

'I don't negotiate with scum. You're a lying son of a bitch and a wanted criminal. You murdered the sheriff of this town along with a score of innocent cowboys. Now you're trying to frame my boy for a killing he didn't commit. I'm doing what any decent law-abiding citizen would do and taking a killer off the streets. No one will blame me for hanging an out-of-control murderer. Take him.'

The smoke curling from the cigar mingled with the smoke of the fuse as Dillon brought the two together. As Hornstone's men moved forward he tossed the smouldering cigar on to the paper confession on Grant's lap. The gunmen were pulling Dillon away from Grant and he made a show of fighting them. They easily overpowered him and hustled him towards the door.

'You lying bastard, Hornstone,' Dillon yelled over his shoulder. 'May you roast in hell for all the misery you brought to this territory.'

Grant was frantically brushing at the cigar while at the same time trying to rescue the confession. He was yelling incoherently as his father moved up to stand beside him. His yells abruptly stopped as Stirling slapped him across the face.

'Must I always clean up your mess. . . ?' was all Dillon heard before he was pushed outside.

He was doing his own yelling while he struggled ineffectually in the grip of the two gunnies as they pushed him into the road.

'Get a rope. We got to hang this son of a bitch.'

Someone tossed a coiled lariat towards them. As the man on Dillon's right stretched out to catch the rope his captive crashed into him, causing him to miss. The lariat landed on the street.

'Goddamn!' yelled the cowboy, as he bent down to recover the rope.

At that moment something blew the door of the Bottom Dollar into the street. The windows exploded also, showering the riders gathered outside the saloon with shards of glass. There was instant pandemonium as horses panicked and reared and kicked and some broke loose and galloped away from the noise. Some cowboys indolently sitting atop their mounts were thrown into the street.

Dillon booted the cowboy bending to retrieve the lariat and the man staggered off balance and went down. Dillon swung round and smashed his fist into the face of the second guard, who had turned round when the dynamite went off. The man staggered back and Dillon went after him, punching him to the ground.

Quickly he snatched the man's pistol from his holster and turned in time to see his other escort scrabbling for his weapon. Dillon lashed out with his boot and caught the man on his elbow. Then bent over and smashed the barrel of his gun over the man's head. He swung round and did the same to the final guard as he was trying to scramble back on his feet.

The street was a scene of panicked horses and cowboys struggling to calm the beasts. A man staggered out of the broken doors of the saloon. He was hatless, his shirt was torn and blood was pouring from a head wound.

'Mr Hornstone's dead,' he yelled. 'The boss is dead – and Grant as well.'

There was a disordered rush towards the saloon. In the general panic and confusion Dillon slipped away, leaving his escorts stretched out in the dirt. He caught up the reins of a cow pony tethered to a hitching rail. No one took any notice of the fugitive as he led the pony down the street and away from the turmoil in front of the saloon.

Men were crowding on the boardwalk in front of the ruined building, peering in through the broken windows and the smashed front doors, anxious to view the carnage inside.

Dillon climbed aboard and nudged the pony to a canter. The animal was eager to get away from the noise and confusion in the main street of Gainsborough.

32

For the second time since coming to Gainsborough Tim Dillon stood in the cemetery. Unlike the previous occasion, this time he was not alone. Amelia Huger was there and Marshal Alex Tobin, who had been sent out from Preston to restore some legitimacy to the law office that had been so much abused during the reign of Hornstone. As well as these three, the cemetery was crowded with mourners. They were the citizens of the town come to attend the funeral of Amelia's son, Raoul. The preacher officiating at the funeral was delivering the final oration.

'There is much sorrow here at this burial. All too brief was Raoul's life. He did not deserve the death he received at the hands of wicked men. We, the citizens of

Gainsborough, share in the guilt that surrounds his death. We are saddened and ashamed that in the hour of her need Amelia did not receive the help from us that might have prevented the tragedy that befell her and her family. Let us hope that in time she will find it in her heart to forgive us for our weakness.

'Amelia showed great courage and fortitude in standing up to the iniquitous men who wrought such terrible devastation on her family. Let us not forget that Edward and Raoul were victims, not only of those who wrought such violence in their lives, but they were also victims of our own cowardice. In the same manner that Our Lord Jesus forgave the men who crucified him, so too do we pray that the Huger family will forgive the citizens of Gainsborough who have gathered here today to pay their respects to the deceased in a spirit of humility and shame. Amen.'

The preacher took a small trowel and sprinkled dirt into the grave. He turned to Amelia and handed her the trowel. Dillon was next to sprinkle dirt followed by Marshal Tobin. As the lawman handed back the small tool the preacher spoke again.

'Mrs Huger, on behalf of the citizens of Gainsborough I offer our condolences and ask if you would permit them to show their remorse by allowing them to perform this last small act for your dead family.'

Amelia looked around at the crowded cemetery and nodded. One by one the citizens shuffled forward, murmuring condolences, not able to meet her eyes; each taking a handful of dirt and sprinkling it into the grave. It took a long time but eventually it was done.

Annie Grimly, the landlady of the boarding house, nodded to Dillon who had stayed very briefly at her place.

'I've prepared a meal for you and Mr Dillon,' she told Amelia. 'I would be honoured if you would attend when you are ready.'

'Thank you. That is most thoughtful of you.'

The cemetery cleared, leaving Tim and Amelia alone. Two men leaning on their shovels stood some distance apart, waiting for the mourners to go before filling in the grave.

'Shall we?' Tim asked.

'I suppose we should go and have that meal we are invited to.'

The couple turned and walked into town. People they encountered raised their hats to Amelia and nodded respectfully to Dillon. The dining room at the boarding house was deserted when they arrived.

'I've refused all other bookings until you have dined,' Annie explained.

'That was thoughtful but unnecessary,' Amelia said.

They sat at the table while the landlady served up roast chicken and potatoes and gravy followed by apple pie and cream. It was only as they sat at the meal they realized how hungry they were. Since coming back to Gainsborough in the company of Marshal Tobin and his deputies there had been no time nor thought for food as they settled Amelia's affairs.

'What do you plan to do now?' Amelia asked as they sat leisurely drinking coffee.

'I ain't had time to figure that far ahead,' Tim replied vaguely. 'With Dexter dead my interests in Gainsborough are about done. What about you?'

'I suppose I should go back East to my family. Like you, there's nothing to keep me here.'

'I'd like to keep in touch.' He stared into his coffee. 'That is if you wouldn't mind.'

There was a long silence before she spoke again. 'I'd like that very much.'

156

Before they could continue Annie came bustling into the room.

'I got a message from Marshal Tobin. He'd like for to see Mr Dillon down at the jailhouse.'

'I'll come now.'

Tim stood and looked down at Amelia, thinking how beautiful she looked even in the dark clothing she had donned for the funeral.

'I'll come with you.'

They found the marshal at the desk behind which, until recently, Sheriff Purdy had dispensed his twisted brand of law.

'Howdy, ma'am, howdy Dillon, take a seat.'

They sat on two rickety chairs, wondering what the lawman had to tell them.

'Dillon, have you made any plans as to what you are going to do?'

Tim shook his head. 'Amelia and I were just discussing that very thing. Why'd you ask?'

The marshal leaned back in his chair and took out his tobacco sack.

'You mind if I smoke, Mrs Huger?'

'No not at all. Please go ahead.'

The lawman began building his cigarette and Tim took out his own makings.

'I've been looking over the situation here in Gainsborough,' Marshal Tobin said as he struck a lucifer. 'Seems to me this town has had no effective law for some time.' His roll-up was glowing now and he blew out the match along with a plume of smoke. 'Judge Peters gave me instructions to review the state of affairs and appoint a sheriff to take charge until he could come here himself and make it legal and permanent.'

Tim lit his own cigarette, wondering why the lawman

was talking to him about such matters.

'The only suitable candidate for the job as far as I can see is you, Dillon. You more or less singlehanded ended the lawlessness of Hornstone. So I'm putting your name forward for the job of sheriff.'

Dillon's smoke went down the wrong way and for a few minutes he couldn't reply as he took a fit of coughing.

'Me? I don't know the first thing about law and order,' he wheezed.

'Dillon, I need you to take this job. If you ain't sure it can be on a temporary basis. But at least you could work at it till the judge gets across here. Then if you change your mind or whatever there's no harm done and you'd be doing me and this town a big favour.'

'I don't know. I hadn't planned on hanging around.' Dillon looked up at Amelia and she was smiling back at him. 'What?' he asked.

'I think you'd make a wonderful sheriff. And perhaps if you decide to stay and take the job I might stay also.'

Dillon found there was something interfering with his breathing. He put it down to the smoke he'd swallowed.

'You'd stay!' he managed to say, beginning to feel a mite light-headed.

'Yes, with you as sheriff I'd feel very safe. After all, you have been looking after me for the past while.'

Dillon went red, unsure what was going on, but he couldn't take his eyes off Amelia and that devastating smile of hers.

'Humph!' The marshal cleared his throat and brought Dillon's attention back to him. 'There's a house to go with the job'

'What!'

'The house will easily accommodate you and if you had it in mind to take a wife. . . .'

The marshal trailed off, watching Dillon's face becoming a deeper shade of red. Suddenly he stood.

'The first thing I'm ordering you to do as your potential boss is to tell this little lady how you feel about her. Then ask her if she would consider staying in Gainsborough to help you settle into your new job. I'm going outside for a moment. When I come back in again I expect you to have come to some conclusion as to your future.'

Left alone with Amelia, Dillon felt unaccountably shy, staring down at his boots.

'Tim.'

He looked up. Amelia was smiling and his heart started that curiously strange pounding again. She stood and held out her hands. Obediently he stood also and took her hands in his.

'It seems to me that Marshal Tobin believes the sheriff's job comes with a wife. Do you have anyone in mind?'

He was lost in her eyes.

When Marshal Tobin peeked into the office again the couple were locked in each other's arms. He nodded in a self-satisfied way.

'Seems as if I might just have got myself a sheriff, after all,' he muttered, and carefully closed the door behind him.